ESCAPEES
&
FEVERED MINDS

David Owain Hughes

A HellBound Books Publishing LLC Book
Houston TX

A HellBound Books LLC
Publication

Cover and art design Kevin Enhart
Edited by Jonathan Edward Ondrashek

www.hellboundbookspublishing.com

Printed in the United States of America

I'd like to dedicate this one to *Richard Laymon* – a man who has not only helped inspire me, but many others like me! A true legend of the genre.

Also by David Owain Hughes
Novels, Novellas and Short Story Collections:

All-Wound Up
Wind-Up Toy
Wind-Up Toy: Broken Plaything
Wind-Up Toy: Chaos Rising
White Walls and Straitjackets
Escapees and Fevered Minds
Choice Cuts
Walled In
Man-Eating Fucks
The Rack & Cue
Collision Course
Granville
Home Improvements
Puckered

Anthologies:
Shadows and Teeth Vol.3
Trapped Within
Hell of a Guy
Unleashing the Voices
Rejected for Content Vol. 4, 5 & 6
Crossroads in the Dark Vol.1 & 2
Fifty Shades of Slay
How to Cook a Baby
Madame Movora's Tales of Terror
Big Book of Bootleg Horror Vol. 1, 2 & 3
Shopping List
Depraved Desires
Easter Eggs and Bunny Boilers
Bah! Humbug!
Slashing Through the Snow
VS Vol. 1 & 2
Black Candy
Into the Abyss

Compiled & Edited Anthologies:
What Goes Around
Man Behind the Mask

Fuck the Rules

ESCAPEES
&
FEVERED MINDS

INTRODUCTION

Escapees and Fevered Minds continues the dark, twisted and wildly imaginative adventures of several larger-than-life characters introduced in *White Walls and Straightjackets* by David Owain Hughes.

Not to worry if you haven't read the first book; you will thoroughly enjoy this sequel as a stand-alone novel. However, I suspect that once you've finished *Escapees and Fevered Minds,* you'll race to pick up the previous book.

If you enjoy your horror on the more extreme side, then Hughes is your man. Not only because he fearlessly and unapologetically explores the more disturbing side of the genre, but also because he is clearly having a jolly good time telling this story. And in turn, we do too.

Make no mistake, Hughes holds nothing back and revels in taking his readers into a splatter-filled heart of darkness, and he doesn't shy away from gore, over-the-top violence, graphic sexual deviance and profanity.

In the hands of lesser authors, extreme horror tales such as this often risk falling victim to their excesses. But Hughes is a talented author, and his ability to navigate the surplus of gore and violence with solid storytelling is deceptive in how easy he makes it look. He understands that pacing, the build-up of suspense and intriguing characters are just as essential as the disturbing elements of the plot.

It is a testament to the lucidness of Hughes' writing that, although the narrative slips back and forth between past and present, and an intriguing use of flashback within flashback and hallucinatory states, the reader never loses sight of where they are in the story.

He has created a dark world indeed, and yet his delight in the subject matter comes through, often in healthy doses of tongue-in-cheek dialogue and an atmosphere of the blackest humor. *Escapees* is a wild and bloody rollercoaster of a novel.

For those brave souls willing to take an excursion through the undeniably twisted imaginings of David Owain Hughes, you are in for a blood-drenched treat. Just make sure to bring your raincoat and galoshes--it's going to get deliciously messy.

- *Taylor Grant, Bram Stoker Award Nominated Author*

PREVIOUSLY...

"Ten years yesterday since you came into my life," she said to him whilst looking in the mirror to apply her make-up. "And look at us now. Performing at the Pavilion in Porthcawl – hardly Las Vegas, is it? I'm beginning to think Khan was full of it when I went to him with my problems all those years ago. Fame, fortune and happiness he promised me. What a joke!

"All I have to show for myself is you, a tatty career, the tattoo he gave me, and a blood trail that will have me doing porridge for the rest of my life if the police should ever catch up with us. It makes my degree and ambition look like a bloody gag. I wanted it all, Harry. The world. Not backstreet gigs in the armpit of nowhere."

Crystal put her eye shadow wand down and picked up her lipstick to rouge her pouty lips.

I'm pushing my luck talking to him this straight, she thought. He's clearly apprehensive about tonight's performance, as he's not talking, just watching me, happy with the view of my half-naked body, no doubt.

Dirty sod. She giggled on the inside, managing to keep the smirk off her face.

He looks so sweet in his bellboy outfit.

Damn it. She couldn't help talking straight. She felt aggrieved. Let down. It wasn't Harry's fault; she just needed to vent, even if she was venting on the wrong person.

"I mean, I can't really complain, Harry." Finishing with the lipstick and picking up her hairbrush, she continued speaking. "You coming into my life was great. I couldn't have wished to meet a more handsome, intelligent, adorable and loving man as yourself. You gave me confidence – taught me to love and respect myself. You brought out the superior creativeness that was hiding within me. The Crystal-*ness*.

"Changing my name was the best thing I ever did! When you brought Crystal out of me Harry, the old me, the Christine Saunders, died. Along with all my inadequacies I had towards my performance work."

With her hair and make-up complete, she stood and eyed herself in the mirror. She wore light brown stockings, fastened by a suspender belt. Her panties were white, with matching bra.

"Shall I put the dress on, Harry?" she teased, letting a schoolgirl giggle go as she bit her finger in a provocative way. "You haven't taken your eyes off me since I sat in front of the mirror." Smiling, she turned and plucked her red 1940s Paris dress off the hanger on the back of her changing room door. She started to slip into it.

"I think we should blow Porthcawl after tonight, Harry. I think the more distance we put between the Rhondda and us would be for the better. We could head to London and make lots of money there. Hell, we may even end up on Broadway!

"Harry, please say something? I know you're nervous about tonight's show, but it's going to be different this time. We won't have snooty judges passing comments on us or running us down in the papers. And if they do, then we'll deal with it just like we did in the Rhondda."

She went to him, knelt before him and put her hands on his knees, resting her head in his lap. "Hold me, Harry." She felt his hand on her back. "Ah, that's nice. Tell me it will be okay, Harry. Please!" The gentle breeze in her ear from his whispers made her skin prickle.

"It's because of you, Harry. It's because of you all this started. From the moment you came to me and helped me see my parents for what they were. They did nothing but hold me back." Tears threatened to come. "They didn't want me to do performing arts at uni. They thought it was a waste of time. They never loved me like they loved Sam. Removing them from my life was the right decision. Burning that church down with them inside was right.

"God, I can still see it now – how the flames looked as they climbed the old stone walls. How the screaming from inside made me smile and giggle with nervous fright at what I had done. The smell of burning flesh had poisoned the air as the grey clouds of smoke filled the summer skies.

"Blaming it all on Sam had been genius. She may have only been a child, but she deserved what she got. Being locked up in that asylum will teach her. My God, it felt good! I felt liberated. Exorcised. She shouldn't have been such a fucking mammy and daddy's girl. You made me see sense, Harry.

"I was in two minds when I was holding that box of matches. But when I threw them and lit the fire, I knew I'd done the right thing. That was the start to my—

our—career and the life we now have together. You're all I need, and ever will need."

She got up, looked down on Harry's small wooden frame, picked him up and cradled him in her left arm. "My little bellboy," she said, grabbing the empty suitcase by her side.

Tonight they would start the show off with her as the hotel customer, disgruntled at the fact the bellboy has been rude to her in more ways than one.

"Oh, Harry. You look so cute," she said, walking out of her dressing room door with a big smile on her face. "Broadway will be our next stop. You'll see, Harry."

"Well, I don't know about you, Harry, but I thought tonight's performance went down very well indeed," Crystal said, setting Harry down on his chair in the corner of the dressing room.

She flicked a switch on the wall by the door, which activated the twenty or so light bulbs around her large dressing room mirror. She then turned the main overhead light off, casting Harry and most of the room in shadow.

"Here you go, my dear," she said, bending over to hand Harry a fat cigar. She lit it for him when it was in his mouth. "Did you have fun tonight?"

"I always have fun when you get your tits out, woman!" he said, his voice harsh. "Now poor me a fucking Scotch."

"Oh, Harry," she said, moving over to the mirror and pulling her chair out. "We don't have any Scotch, but I'll do you one when we get back to The Sea Bank?" She stood facing Harry and slowly undid her dress. She slipped it down her curvaceous body inch by inch, gradually revealing her bra and then panties, and finally the tops of her stockings.

Harry said nothing, just chuffed on his cigar in his black recess. The bright burning end of the Cuban was evidence he was still there, along with thin strands of smoke which floated to the ceiling.

"You like, baby?" she said, putting on a dirty voice. Stepping out of her dress, which was now around her ankles, she stood before him and fondled her bra-covered breasts. She knew it was driving him wild; as she started to propel her hair, a grunt of approval came from his direction.

Stopping, she turned her back and sat down. Looking in the glass, she smiled.

"You fucking prick tease," he hissed.

"You can have me later, my dear. When we get back to our room." Opening a drawer to her left, Crystal took out a small bottle of nail polish remover, along with a slender packet of facial wipes and a box of tissues.

"I noticed a lot of the same faces out in the crowd tonight," Harry stated. "We got a following here. Maybe we shouldn't be in such a rush to leave."

"But—"

"But nothing," he barked. "We got it good here. With good money and a good room at that fancy hotel the organisers have us holed up in." He took a fat drag on his cigar. "Let's forget London for now. We've only done a few months here."

"What do you suggest?" Crystal asked.

"That we build up some cash, enough to get us to London and keep us there. Word is spreading about our show." Another drag, followed by a wheeze and a cough.

"I wish you wouldn't smoke those things, Harry. They're no good for your chest."

"Yes, Mammy," he mocked. "Those cigs you used to smoke before I came along certainly did nothing to harm your chest, girlie!"

"Hmm," she said, balling up a used facial wipe before binning it. She plucked another from the pack and wiped at her face once again, removing the last of her make-up. "Okay, okay. We'll stash some cash then bail as soon as we have enough."

"Good, and stop fucking worrying about the police catching up with us. Those dumb fucks are none the wiser – they haven't got a clue who they're looking for!"

"Okay, Harry," she said, throwing the second wipe away.

"Right, that's me just about..."

A newspaper clipping, which was pinned to the back of her dressing room door, caught her attention. "What the hell is that?" she said, fully turning to look at it. Not being able to see the headline on the clipping, she firstly tried to bend forward and squint before giving up and walking over to it. The *click-click* of her heels pierced the silence in the medium-sized room.

Harry watched.

When she was point-blank range with the clipping, she started to read it nice and loud, so Harry could hear her.

June 27 2012 Page 1

Three Flee In Asylum Meltdown Unofficial report by P.I. Ty Schwamberger

NOT PRINTED

Photo of Castell Hirwaun

Few things can terrify residents more than mental patients escaping from an asylum. But that's exactly what happened recently at Castell Hirwaun. The actual details of how the escape took place are sketchy at this time, but this reporter has learned, from a trusted source within the hospital's sacred walls, the names and some background of the three individuals who are now on the run.

Being the standup reporter that I am, I won't name names of who gave me this information, but I have been fortunate to receive copies of all three individual patient assessment forms. Below is what we know about these sick persons.

The first patient is simply known as "Santa Klaws". From what I've learned, this isn't because Castell Hirwaun likes to give cute nicknames to their patients. Oh, no. More, because no one knows his real name or background. In Mr. Santa Klaws' patient assessment form, it states he recites the words to "'Twas the Night Before Christmas" incisively and likes to keep to himself. However, when provoked, he can instantly turn mean and injure and even kill the hospital staff who are only there to help him. Mr. Klaws was taken to Castell Hirwaun shortly after being apprehended at the scene of a grisly crime, which we have little to no details about.

The second patient who escaped is Norm Nathanial Jenkins. There is more known about Mr. Jenkins than Mr. Klaws. In fact, years ago, I reported about the death of his wife, Angharad. By all accounts Mr. Jenkins was a productive member and well liked by the community prior to having a mental breakdown after witnessing his wife's death while mountain climbing together. Since that time, he has taken on a second personality and fallen into a deep depression. This horrible loss led Mr. Jenkins to begin murdering people in an attempt to "rebuild" his wife's damaged body. It is unclear why or in what capacity Mr. Klaws and Mr. Jenkins were working together prior to the escape.

The third and final escapee is a Miss Samantha Saunders. From what I learned on her assessment form, Miss Saunders has suffered from mental disorders since a very young age, spending time in Rosemary's Hospital. Miss Saunders has been at Castell Hirwaun for the past ten years. She began her time in the mental hospitals after killing her parents, along with several others, after she set fire to a chapel one afternoon. From all eyewitness accounts, it was in fact Samantha who committed the ghastly deed; however, she tried to make local authorities believe it was her older sister. She was committed to Rosemary's Hospital the day of her parents' funerals.

You, I and we have lived and worked in this community for years. We try to do good by one another, never causing any harm. Unfortunately, we all know there are some out there who suffer from mental illness and/or are just plain psychos (to use a non-politically correct term) that don't care about others' well-being. We all try to live our lives without looking over our shoulder, not worrying if something is going to creep up behind us and stab us in the spine with a dirty knife, but, tragically, it does happen in today's world.

This brings me back to these three individuals who escaped from Castell Hirwaun. It really makes you wonder if something sinister is going on behind those old stone walls... Is the medical staff truly qualified to run the hospital and take proper care of its patients? Will the day come when the patients are running the asylum... Or are they already? Is this how the escape happened or was it simply a slip up?

At this point your guess, my fine readers, is as good as mine.

Let's just hope authorities can find the three individuals before they cause harm to someone new.

Until they are apprehended, I suggest you keep your windows and doors locked tight at all times of the day and night.

Oh... and remember to keep a watchful eye over your shoulder.

Good Luck!

With shaking hands, Crystal unpinned the clipping and started reading the rest of the news story.

"Speak up, woman. I can't hear your mutterings!"

"Sorry, Harry. It says here that Sam and two others have escaped from Castell Hirwaun. The reports on the escapees are 'sketchy.' Jesus, what if she heads here,

Harry? Tries to track me down? She said she would…kill me. That…that…"

"That's not going to fucking happen, dummy. And if it does, we'll *fix* her."

Crystal looked at Harry, and although she couldn't see his face, she knew by the tone of his voice how serious he was.

"I…I…" She felt something taped to the back of the thin sheet of paper. On turning it over, she found a slender white envelope with "READ ME" written on it in black. The lines were thick, suggesting a marker pen had been used.

"Oh, God, Harry. There's a letter here, too!"

"Open it. *Now!*"

Her fingers feverishly tore the envelope apart, and she snatched the letter from inside. Again, she read aloud.

Dear Crystal,

I'm throwing a dinner party tomorrow night at 20.00. The gathering will be held at 379 Eagle Moss Av, Porthcawl. I'd like you to come. Harry, too.

As you know, your sister and a few others have escaped their prison. They too will be attending my revelry. I think it will be in your best interest to attend, as you'll get to meet another very important guest and not just Sam.

Dearest,
Wadsworth

"What the fuck is that about?"

"I have no idea," Crystal said, a quiver in her voice.

"What's that address again?" Harry asked.

"What?"

"The address for the house, for fuck sake, girl!"

"Oh, erm, I'm not...Oh, no, wait, here it is: 379 Eagle Moss Av, Porthcawl."

"Eagle Moss? Sounds like something out of a goddamn Hammer Horror. Who's our host, Peter Cushing? Vincent Price?! Throw it all away, Crystal. It's got to be some sort of wind up."

"But what about this news article? It's got yesterday's date on it."

"And?" Harry said, anger rising in his voice. "It's got 'NOT PRINTED' written on it. That suggests it's unofficial. Someone's having a wind-up, that's all!"

"If it isn't, it means that Sam has been on the run for the past twenty-four hours. She could be in town by now."

"And what's she going to do?"

Crystal stared at the letter and clipping as goose pimples prickled her flesh, making her skin crawl. She raised her eyes and looked into the darkness where Harry sat. "Do you think we should attend? It says there will be another guest there that I would *want* to meet."

"Yeah, I think we should check it out. Go and play a stupid fucking game of *Come Dine with Me*, or worse still, *Cluedo*!"

A smile crept across Crystal's face, but only momentarily, as fear came sneaking back. What if the letter and clipping was for real, she wondered?

LATER THAT EVENING...

After taking Harry and all their gear back to the Sea Bank Hotel, and fixing Harry and herself a Scotch, they sat and drank whilst chewing the fat over the letter and clipping. After four or five whiskeys, Harry fell into a deep sleep, leaving Crystal to tread the boards of their room with a frantic nature.

I need to clear my head, she thought, before I smash this room apart. Looking out the huge bay windows of the room, which overlooked the beach, she could hear rolling waves crash against the waiting rocks.

The lights to the circus to her left then caught her attention. She'd seen the carnival dubbed *The Circus of Fear* roll into town a few days ago – as a child, she'd loved the fair, and had even thought about running away to join up.

Looking at the clock on the nightstand next to her bed, she didn't think eleven-thirty was too late for a stroll along the promenade, and to take in the childish attraction. Maybe it would help clear her mind.

"Where are you, Sam?" she asked under her breath. "Are you in town? You're bound to be coming for me. You're hoping I'll take the bait of that letter. Was it you that really sent it? You promised you'd kill me that day back at the asylum…"

She grabbed her leather jacket off the back of the chair, slipped it on, then made sure Harry was sleeping before heading out the door. By the sound of his heavy snoring, he'd be out until morning, she decided.

Walking from her hotel down to the promenade, Crystal only encountered the odd few people. Some were chatting couples that shared a bag of chips, while other couples came spewing out of pubs, laughing and joking.

She was in no mood for pleasantries. Her mind was a whirlwind of thoughts– she feverishly scanned the faces of people she saw on the streets and alleys that she ventured down. Sam, I know you're here, and if not, you soon will be, she thought.

A shiver clawed its way up her spine.

Looking behind her, the dark street was empty. Nobody lurked.

Would Sam plunge steel into her sister's turned back? The callous bitch probably would, after what I've done to her. Why is this happening now? Just as Harry and I settle somewhere away from all the death and trouble, this has to happen. Maybe going to see her that day had been a bad move. It had riled Sam. But Crystal had no idea this would happen, that Sam would break out of Castell Hirwaun.

Sighing, she stopped walking and stood in front of a coin-operated telescope. For twenty pence, you could look through and out over the sea to spy on the little vessels, yachts, tankers, cargo boats and people playing on the beach by day.

She drank in the air, looked about her, and spotted the fair off in the near distance. The place jumped with life. The brightly coloured neon lights and lively dance music was a beacon for thrill-seekers and kids alike. And for some reason, it was calling her, too.

So, onward she went, attempting to walk in well-lighted areas.

On the beach, she saw a barrel spitting flames. Teenagers sat around it playing loud rock music whilst drinking beer.

She had a pang of envy as she passed them by. Oh, how things could have been so different, she thought. Looking about her, memories came flooding back from the days she used to work in Porthcawl as a dancer. Bunnies, the club she had once worked at, had been pulled down years ago.

Those were simpler times, she thought.

The seaside town had become a ghost town of sorts – many buildings were now boarded up. Pubs had closed down. The fair seemed to be the only thriving business left. It hadn't been like that when Crystal had first worked the place.

As she neared the amusement park, the more the smells stuffed her nostrils: the stench of candyfloss, seafood, hotdogs and burgers. Sounds of meat and onions sizzling collided with whoops of joy, thudding disco music and lots of screaming and laughter as various rides tossed and threw their riders about in their seats.

As Crystal got closer still, flocks of people seemed to come from nowhere. The Cabin/Dolly Bar, situated just outside the fairground entrance, was full. Drunkards lined the outside of the shoddy, wipe-your-feet-on-the-way-out watering hole, and whistled and eyed Crystal as she passed by. The butcher knife she had on the inside of her coat felt snug and heavy.

"Fuck off," she snarled in their direction. Some looked away; others answered with an "oooh." "Fucking lowlifes," she muttered, entering through the huge iron gates to the fair.

The voice of an MC blazed out of his megaphone as he hammered on about "Nobody walks away a loser. We have a winner every time!" It was difficult to pinpoint where it was coming from, such was the din about her. Above Crystal's head, the Beach Party ride flew into the air, its passengers screaming as the ride went full circle.

Piles of teens graced the inside of the fair – some were trying their luck at the stalls, which promised "A winner every time!" Crystal watched grown men throwing balls at cans as they tried in vain to topple an aluminium pyramid for a prize.

After passing the stalls, Crystal sauntered by Madam Carla's tent. She was a fortune-teller who looked older than Porthcawl itself. "Come in, child!" a decrepit voice beckoned from beyond the gloom. "Let Madam Carla tell you what you need!" she whispered.

Laughing, Crystal moved on.

She didn't know where she was heading as she pushed through the crowds and kept her eyes peeled for an attack she felt *was* coming. I think that's why I came out, she thought. To confront the bitch. This will be her chance, if indeed that letter isn't bullshit. Well, let's be having you.

Crystal turned a hundred-and-eighty degrees slowly, spotting nothing unusual in the crowds. She faced front and walked on, the big top at the far end of the ground now grabbing her full attention. As she drew closer, she could hear the ringmaster address the crowd and crack his whip. The massive, dull-coloured tent of blacks and whites felt foreboding. She peeled one giant flap back and poked her head inside. She cast her eyes on the stilted ringmaster, who bore a top hat and macabre make-up.

"*Ladies and gentlemen, boys and girls, prepare to be shocked and disturbed by the Circus of Fear...Dear parents, please do mind your children, as some of our acts do tend to bite, eat and devour our smaller members of the crowd – especially Mr. Tickles and his freakish assistants, Miss Sideshow Necrotic and Miss Sideshow Nightshade...*"

The inside of the tent plunged into darkness, much to the squeals and shrieks of delight and terror from the audience members. Crystal's insides felt cold as she transfixed her eyes on the opening curtains at the opposite end of the tent.

She felt like a little girl again, standing there watching with her mouth agape as plumes of smoke burped out of the opening, followed by the whine and growl of a car engine. This was followed by a deafening, sinister laugh, which filled the entirety of the tent and surrounding area.

Close by, she heard a child cry over the raucous sounds, "I want to go home, Mammy. *Now*!"

Then, thundering heavy metal music engulfed the tent, replacing the sound of the car and horrid laughter.

I sense the sweat burst on my temple
Is it me or is it shadows fox-trotting on my walls
Is this a vision or is it now
Is this a delusion or normal what I see before my sight

She knew the song, but the words were wrong. Disjointed somehow, like the man-clown who drove his car out of the parting curtains. A woman clad in purple was tied to the bonnet. This was no ordinary clown's car, she thought, where a million clowns get out of a tiny vehicle, which then falls to pieces after the door is closed with too much enthusiasm.

There was something much more sinister and evil about this clown who drove the roofless car. The bodywork was painted black, with a huge skull and crossbones on the bonnet. Crystal took a step backward, feeling the clown's soulless-looking eyes on her. Drinking her in. Roaming her body. Did he know her? Did she know him?

No, she didn't think so.

His teeth appeared to be needle sharp. The blacks and whites around his eyes made his sockets seem empty. Bottomless pits. She gulped, slowly letting the flap go. "Just walk away," she said aloud. "Go back to Harry. It's getting…"

A flyer stuck to the canvas tent flap caught her attention. "What's this…" she started, plucking the mini poster free. She held it out in front of her and read.

SEE THE AMAZING *MISS NIGHTSHADE* – THE WORLD'S ONLY KNOWN VAMPIRE…THE EBONY WONDER IS AS STUNNING AS SHE IS DEADLY…SEE HER SINK HER FANGS INTO MEMBERS OF THE AUDIENCE, AND PRAY IT'S NOT YOU, AS SHE RECRUITS FOR HER ARMY OF THE NIGHT…

Miss Sideshow Nightshade xx

"*You!* The one by the entrance. Get in here!" barked the clown over the speakers, his voice replacing the music.

Crystal let the flyer flutter to the floor.

The clown had now parked in the centre of the big top. His sidekick, the female jester, was now standing on the bonnet – she lashed at the dusty ground with her chains. She licked her lips and gyrated her body to the metal music, which had kicked back in.

Crystal felt a thousand eyes on her as her cheeks flushed. She walked in and took a seat.

His act was lurid. Much worse than mine and Harry's, she thought. This clown, this Mr. Tickles, along with his partner, Miss Sideshow Necrotic, is sick. She loved it. They kept her amused and entertained. Crystal squealed with delight as lone youngsters from the crowd took to centre stage as volunteers for different stunts and performances, never to return to their seats. Where had they gone? Was it real blood on the floor?

Crystal didn't care. The sadistic horror she saw unfold before her was giving her ideas for her own act with Harry. She needed to meet this clown after the show. She needed to talk with him, but she didn't know why. Crystal wasn't looking for any creative ideas. She had plenty. There was just something about this guy.

Most of the audience members had walked out by the grand finale, giving Crystal her opportunity to get to the clown before he left the tent.

Fighting her way through the remainder of the audience, Crystal got within earshot of a fan asking Mr. Tickles for his autograph, which was met by a low, growling, "Piss off, kid." It was spat into the teen's general direction. "Before I bite your face off, and feed the rest of you to Custard!" Mr. Tickles added, looking up from the floor.

Mr. Tickles, who was well over six feet tall, turned his back to pick up his bag of tricks – a Hessian sack with *Tricks* marked across the side of it in black – and

Miss Sideshow Necrotic's chain. He then proceeded to move towards the part of the tent he'd emerged from earlier that evening, with Sideshow crawling on her hands and knees behind him. This amused Crystal, along with the fact that they were now the only three left inside the big top.

"*The Last Freak Show on Earth....*" Crystal whispered.

The massive clown stopped dead in his tracks, but Sideshow kept on moving, until her master forcefully pulled her backward by her constraint. A mass choking fit ensued, which almost drowned out Mr. Tickles' low belly growls.

"I thought you seemed familiar," Crystal continued, almost whimpering. This was the first person to ever truly scare the living shit out of her. This guy even made Harry look like a choirboy.

Crystal could hear Sideshow snicker in the shadows. The sly laughter made her think of a snake's hiss as it slithered towards its prey. She went numb in the shadow cast by Mr. Tickles as he fully faced her. His needle-like teeth, which were stained red, shone in the half-light.

"*Huh*?!" he uttered. Saliva glistened on his chin. "Come again?" he said flatly.

Nothing but the cold rattle of Sideshow's chain broke the silence as Crystal thought of what to say next. She discreetly backed away whilst sliding a hand inside her leather jacket. She closed her fingers around the haft of the butcher knife.

"I...I..."

"Spit it out, child!" he grumbled. There was a stale smell of whiskey on his breath.

"I...I..."

"Maybe she wants a balloon?" Sideshow chirped in, snickering some more.

"Maybe," Mr. Tickles said. "Is that it, pumpkin? You want a balloon or a lollypop?"

"I said," Crystal finally asserted herself, "'*The Last Freak Show on Earth*.' You used to be Mr. Sugar Giggles."

His brow furrowed and his eyes seemed to narrow. "I *think* you're getting your Chuckles and your Kokos mixed up, lady! Now why don't you walk out of here. Or would you prefer to leave on a stretcher? And that's if you're lucky!"

They were almost nose to nose, with him bent over.

She had him rattled. She knew this was the same clown. The furrows in his forehead were a giveaway. He was dumbstruck, trying to figure out how in the hell he'd been noticed. This guy had disappeared, just like that, after years of performing. She'd loved seeing him at her local fair as a teenager. It was said he'd been put in an asylum long ago…

He'd been a slight inspiration to her.

"I'm right, aren't I? I used to love watching you perform in those days."

"Who the fuck are you? Nobody's called me by that name in years!"

"I could possibly be your worst nightmare then," Crystal said, grinning…

Escapees and Fevered Minds

PREVIOUSLY...

She was cold. Cold and hungry. Her energy levels were near zero. It had been a struggle to keep going. She couldn't remember the last time she'd eaten a good meal, like fish or steak.

The letter she had found in the car had told her to come to Hob's Café. The letter prior to that, which had been slipped into her cell, had told her what was going to happen and what she needed to do.

Dear Samantha,

My lovely Sam.

There's not much time to explain things here in this letter, but I promise to answer all your questions when I see you in a few days' time. At exactly midnight tonight, the power will go down in the asylum and your door will be unlocked. The key in this envelope is a skeleton key, and will aid you in your escape. Within the grounds will be a car. A limo. A driver has been provided. He is

31

forbidden to explain anything to you, so don't bother trying to grill him. Also, there will be another letter awaiting you.

All my love,

Wadsworth

At first, Samantha had been scared. She thought the letter had been a figment of her imagination, that she really was losing her mind. Or was it a dream? The paper and envelope had felt real enough. But then again, her medication played tricks on her, like it had done before.

Regardless, she had waited with held breath inside her box room to see if anything would happen, hoping and praying the letter was authentic. She needed out. Craved freedom.

Time had seemed to stand still, even though she had no concept of it anymore. Day was night, night was day. They had kept her in solitary confinement mostly, usually strapped to a bed. But she had started to behave, played ball, in the hope that they would transfer her to a minimum security wing in time to come.

As these thoughts had danced in her head, her room was plunged into darkness. At first, Sam didn't panic, thinking it was time for 'lights out'. But then she'd heard the panic and upheaval start outside her room.

My God, it's really happening!

She had sprung from her bed, not feeling any terror towards who or what was helping her escape. She just seized the opportunity. And, as the letter had promised, the door was unlocked. In her excitement, Sam had almost forgotten to take the skeleton key with her, which, as stated, opened every barred door from her room to the outside.

Her escape went unnoticed, due to nurses and guards being kept busy by every other patient on her ward. Plus, she had thought, if the power was completely down, all the cameras would be off too.

The corridors and rooms were dimly lit by lights that the backup generator provided for. All main lights were down.

It had taken Sam less than twenty minutes to work her way out of the hospital, and ten more to find the waiting limo. All its windows were blacked out. The exhaust pipe emitted smoke, suggesting the engine was idling.

The driver's window had slid down, and a whisper of a voice came at her. "Get in the back – the doors are unlocked. Thank you."

A shiver glided down her back due to the situation and the coldness of the night. The gentle breeze plastered her prison fatigues, which had the hospital's name stencilled on it, to her body. Behind her, she'd heard the commotion going on inside the hospital walls of Castell Hirwaun.

Sam opened the back door, but before getting in, she had checked to see if anyone was lurking and ready to do her harm. Maybe Crystal.

Why would someone help me escape?

Was it Crystal?

Did she feel bad?

Well, if it is her, then the bitch has made a fatal error in letting me out. I told her I'd kill her.

"In, please," the driver had said.

Sam got in, closed the door and tried to relax. *If it wasn't Crystal, then who? Who cares, I'm out!*

Taped to a shelf holding decanters and glasses was a second letter. This one had "Sam" written across it.

She had ripped the envelope apart.

My lovely Sam,

If you are reading this, then you have made it to the outside untroubled, and are sat in the limo provided. The driver has been instructed to take you to Hob's, which is a café on an old road close to Hirwaun. Once there, the limo will leave you.

You'll then need to go inside and ask for Hob. He is the owner. He will be expecting you and will provide you with everything you need: food, clothes, money and a bus ticket which will see you to Porthcawl. He will also give you a third and final letter. When we do meet, I can promise you that it will be more than worth your while.

One other thing, do help yourself to a Scotch or rum provided in the crystalware.

Warmest,

Wadsworth

After she had finished the letter, the limo pulled off as though the driver had been waiting for her to read it. She poured herself a drink, sat back, and let her thoughts wash over her. Who is this *Wadsworth* fella? she thought. Was it someone she knew? Someone from her past? They'd kept her on some pretty strong meds at the hospital, which meant she'd forgotten a lot of things.

Thirty minutes later, she reached her destination.

And now, looking out the car's window at Hob's, she felt a chill cut a pathway down her back. No lights appeared to be on inside the place, which was understandable. It was gone three A.M.

The car park was deserted save for one other vehicle, which she supposed belonged to the restaurateur.

Anyone could be watching from behind those darkened windows, she thought. I could be walking into a trap. But why would they drag me all the way out here, to a café, just to off me? Hell, the limo driver could have taken me somewhere, then beat, raped and murdered me. No, there was more to this letter game, and she wanted to know what.

Sam got out of the car and limped over to the front door of the café. Behind her, the limo drove away, slowly, but she paid it no attention and knocked lightly on the café's door.

She winced at the loud echo sounds in which it created.

A drone of a voice came from within, causing Sam to gasp and jump back.

"It's open."

The voice sounded hideous. Sly and mean, even.

She pulled the door open at a steady pace, expecting the worst. She felt so weak. As she lamely entered Hob's, the place lit up and the voice spoke again.

"You must be Samantha Saunders? My first of three visitors this evening," the fat man said from his place behind the counter.

"*Three*?" Sam asked, more to herself.

"That's right. I got two more of you to come." He stepped from behind the counter and ushered her to a seat. "Take a load off," he said, placing a plate in front of her. It had a piece of gammon on it, complete with fried egg, slice of pineapple and chunky chips. "Get you something to drink?"

"Er...erm..." Sam felt confused by it all. "Who are you. Are you Hob?"

"Yes, I'm Hob. I'm here to help get you to Porthcawl."

"What? Why? Why Porthcawl?"

"Calm yourself, love," he said, taking her emaciated right hand and patting it. "It's all here in this letter I have for you. Now eat your meal before it gets cold."

"But..."

"Eat up, and read that letter of yours."

"I'll have...a beer if you've got one, Hob. Hell, bring me a jug of the stuff!"

"*Wahahaha*," Hob bellowed, slapping his knee. "Hell, consider it done, lovely."

She eyed him for a moment, then furiously tore into her gammon, stuffing the chips in along with sections of meat until her mouth couldn't fit any more. Her throat struggled to cope with the amount it was being asked to swallow.

Before she opened the envelope to the next letter, Hob placed a sweating jug of ice-cold lager down on the table in front of her. A chilled pint glass was also plonked on the table. Beads of water ran off the jug and soaked through the tablecloth.

"Enjoy. I'll leave you in peace to finish your meal and read your letter. Once you're ready, we'll get you scrubbed and cleaned, then into a fresh set of clothes."

She said nothing, just eyed him as he walked back into what she assumed was the kitchen.

As Sam slowly chewed and rammed more food into her mouth, she looked about her, taking in the American themed restaurant/bar, which had a pool table and a jukebox. Had she the energy and coin, she would have fed the jukebox some money. Instead, she opened her final letter.

Dearest Sam,

I hope my loyal pet Hob is looking after you? You can confide in me when I see you if he hasn't. He's just a pawn that can be easily removed! I'll be waiting for you at 379 Eagle Moss Av, Porthcawl. A party has been arranged, with some very special *guests. One of which will be your sister, Crystal.*

Hob will provide you with evening wear, which I personally picked out for you, along with some clothes to, umm, 'kick around in', shall we say. Also, Hob should provide you with a bus ticket and some, as aforementioned. Come to Porthcawl tonight. I shall be waiting for you, my love.

Warmest,

Wadsworth

"*Crystal*," Sam uttered, then crushed the letter into a ball.

EARLIER THAT WEEK...

Strange things are constantly happening in or around this café, Hob thought as he held the letter open in front of him.

People went missing – staff and customers alike. It had been going on for months. The police said a serial killer was on the loose in the area. That may be true to a point, Hob thought, but most have gone missing due to Bella and me.

But we're not responsible for *all* the disappearances around here, uh-uh. And I most certainly don't kill my staff members, he thought. We mainly kill solo customers who come in and ask for "The Works", and they are normally single or bored married men.

The way Hob and his wife saw it, they were doing the single men a favour by curing them of their loneliness, and the married men's wives a favour by doing away with their debauched and adulterous husbands.

Everyone's a winner, right?

Not only were the men no longer lonely and the wives being made fools of, but Hob had also saved his café, which had been floundering due to money issues. How? Because he served the dead men to his punters. It cut out the cost of buying expensive meats from wholesalers, which in return kept Hob's open for business in these hard times. Everything was running fine.

Or so it had seemed.

Many months had passed since Hob and Bella had started their meat operation in the bowels of their property. The police stopped by every so often to check in on the unsuspecting couple, to inform them of more missing persons and to see if they were okay.

After all, the place was situated out on an old road, with barely any traffic passing through these days. Just loyal customers (mainly truckers and bikers) who knew of its existence.

So all seemed to be running smooth. Then, just this morning, a letter arrives. Unmarked. No stamp. It had been hand delivered.

Hob had found it hanging out of the letterbox like a limp tongue from a mouth. He'd spotted it as soon as he'd flipped the lights on at four A.M. No post ever came that early, and it sure as hell hadn't been there last night at locking up time.

So, from between two and now, the letter had appeared. He'd pulled it from the post slot, which snapped back into place after the offending article had been removed.

Hob had flipped it over and found two words scribed on the chalk-white envelope.

"I KNOW!"

His bladder almost released, but he had managed to pinch it just in time. He could feel a tiny wet patch at the front of his pants. He'd known exactly what the words were referring to. They looked filthy. Dirty, somehow. Like they didn't belong, but did.

They'd caught in his brain and throat.

He was almost too scared to peel the envelope's flap open, let alone take the letter out from inside, but he had. He'd sat on a stool by the counter to read.

Dear Hob,

I know about your filthy secret.

I've known all along, since the day you started your murderous spree to save your failing business.

How could you drag your lovely Bella into such a diseased idea? Were you too scared to take a fall all by yourself, should the police finally find out what you've been up to? Were you not man enough to take charge alone? Bella probably now commands the whole venture and looks after you, you sniffling excuse of a man.

I'm not interested in your inadequacies as a man or a human. All I am interested in is your cooperation and loyalty, and now that I most definitely have your full attention, I am going to explain what it is I expect from you. In return for your help, you will have my silence about your secret.

Hob put the letter down. He was shaking. Shaking badly. He needed a caffeine fix. The percolator had clicked on via its timer and was now boiled and ready. Hob shifted over to it. It was more of a dazed shamble than a walk. His knees felt weak, as though he had just taken a two-minute pounding at the hands of Vladimir Klitchko.

Taking a mug from the rack, he proceeded to fill it with the mud-like liquid. He added four sugars – his norm. Taking a hearty swallow, he let things start to register. There wasn't a panic as such. The authorities hadn't been informed. His and Bella's dirty activities were still their secret, but now this evil fucker was trying to destroy them and everything they had worked hard for.

He needed to calm down before continuing to read the rest of his letter. "Cheeky fucker," Hob said aloud. "Who the fuck does this prick think he is? Getting off on calling me a coward. I'll bash his fucking brains out." With that, he went to the other side of the counter, unhooked the steel bat suspended there, and pulled it up close to him. *Old Rosie* was engraved in the bloodstained steel.

"Old Rosie's no—"

The jukebox kicked in, which was also on a timer.

I lead a life of law-breaking
Filthy acts, completed dirt cheap
Filthy acts, completed dirt cheap
Filthy acts, completed dirt cheap
Filthy acts and they're completed dirt cheap
Filthy acts and they're completed dirt cheap
So you're havin' trouble with your life
You got a busted heart
He's double dealing your best friend
That's when the tears begin to drop

Hob turned, swinging the bat as he went, and smacked his half-full mug off the counter. It sailed through the air and obliterated against the wall next to the jukebox.

His intense panting quickly turned to uncontrolled bouts of laughter as he lowered his bat and cautiously looked about the café. There was nobody there. The car park was empty. Dawn was beginning to break.

He looked at the jukebox, which was aglow with a murky green colour that seemed freaky to him.

Sighing, he put the bat down on the countertop. He then picked up a damp rag and went to the wall to mop it clean. He also picked up the shards of disintegrated mug and placed them in the bin.

Finished with the clean-up, he poured himself another coffee and sat back at the counter, making sure Old Rosie was close by. He continued to read.

Firstly, let me explain: My name is Wadsworth. Who or what I am is of no concern to you. Neither is my real name – Wadsworth is an alias. Secondly, I am holding a 'social gathering' for VIPs. Three of these VIPs will be visiting you.

Whether you know it or not, an asylum by the name of Castell Hirwaun is situated not too far from your establishment, and is home to some very colourful individuals. And that is where the three VIPs will be coming from next week – they'll be visiting you for some good old-fashioned hospitality, before making their way to my home in Porthcawl.

Now, I know you may have some concerns about letting the mad into your home, but they will do you no harm. Just feed, water and bathe them. They'll be on their way before you know it. Later this week, I shall send you a package with clothes, money and bus tickets for the three individuals. I wish for you to present the articles to my guests as they arrive. There will also be letters for each of them.

Once you have done this task for me, I will no longer require your help. You will not hear from me again, and you will be able to rest assured that your secret will die with me. But only *if you do as instructed, Hob.*

Yours sincerely,

Wadsworth

A few days later, as promised, Hob received a parcel via a Royal Mail courier, which he had to sign for.

He'd managed to hide the letter from Bella, but not the parcel. She'd demanded to know what was going on, and had the parcel anything to do with the way he'd been acting the last couple of days?

Hob had caved to his wife, spilling his guts to her the moment they'd closed for the night. She'd been steely throughout what he had to tell her. Bella was not fazed or shaken by it, not like he had been. She held him as he cried. Soothed him as he shook uncontrollably in her arms.

Bella had always been the perfect woman. He'd known that, from the first moment he'd met her. He knew they were meant to be. And he knew she would always be the strong one.

"We'll just do as he wants," Bella coolly told him. "He's not threatening violence or bribery. We'll be fine, you'll see, Hob."

Inside the parcel, packed neatly, were five sets of clothing. One was a spangled black dinner dress with plunging neckline, accompanied by sexy lingerie, an expensive women's watch and a string of beads. There was a tag attached to the dress. It read: "*For Samantha.*"

Next, he pulled out a pair of faded blue jeans, along with a black T-shirt that had a bottle on it. Within the bottle, pink fluid sloshed. Written above the bottle was the word "Poison." These were also "For Samantha", along with underwear but minus accessories.

Followed by those clothes was yet another pair of jeans, these bigger, along with a plain jumper. It had the colour of charcoal. The tag on this read "For Norm"; so too did the dapper male dinner suit that followed. There was also a belt and an expensive men's watch accompanying the gear.

Last in line, and definitely the most bizarre, was a big, black Father Christmas costume. No suit, no jeans, no T-shirt. Just this. On the tag was "For Klaws."

If the situation hadn't have been so fucking crazy, Hob probably would have bellowed with laughter. But it slightly scared him. What type of nut would want a black Santa suit? More disturbing was the thought that the nut was heading his way.

Putting all the clothes to one side, he continued to unpack the satanic parcel. There were three bus tickets and three bundles of cash – one each for the 'VIPs', – along with three letters. Each envelope was scribed with a name: Samantha, Klaws or Norm.

Poking his head out from behind the kitchen door, he looked at Sam. Hob couldn't help but wish one of the men had been first. Somehow, he felt the other two were going to be the most dangerous. But, having said that, Samantha seems placid enough, he thought. That had helped Hob ease his fears somewhat regarding the two men.

I'm glad I managed to persuade Bella to stay out of the way, Hob thought. I don't want her getting hurt if things should turn ugly.

Noting Samantha had finished her food, Hob went over to her. Her plate gleamed from where she had licked it clean. Her jug of beer sat empty.

"Everything okay with the food?" he asked.

"Lovely, thanks," she replied, belching.

Hob was shocked at how polite, tame, and 'normal' she was. She sure didn't look or act like someone that was crazy. I wonder what she did to get herself locked up in that God-awful place?

She was pretty, too. A bit thin, but pretty. He supposed she hadn't been eating much in that asylum, either through her own choice or on account of them starving her. He doubted it was the first of the two, after seeing how she had crammed food into her mouth.

"Erm, would you like to get cleaned up? I have a private bathroom out back. I've placed your clothes and money from Wadsworth in there."

"Who are you, and what part do you have to play in this?" she asked, suddenly turning on him.

He looked stunned. "I...I...I'm not in on any of this, if that's what you think. I had a letter too! A letter telling me about you coming here this evening, and that I was to expect three of you. That I—"

"Who are the other two?" she demanded to know.

"It's another two from the asylum. That's all I know. I swear!"

"Let me see your letter!"

Beads of sweat formed on his forehead. Fear. That's what it was, and it was nestling into the pit of his stomach. It was warm and stabbing, twisting his guts into knots.

"I threw it away last night," he quickly said, hoping his lie would go undetected.

"*Hmm*," she said. "Where's this bathroom?"

"This way." He sighed, relieved that she had dropped the matter so fast. Smiling, he led her to the bathroom, which was fitted with a shower, sink and toilet.

"Here you go. Take as long as you need. I've hung your clothes up on the hook behind the door, and your money and bus ticket are on the laundry basket. You can put your hospital clothes in there, ready for me to burn, along with your ID bracelet and anything else you want gone," he said, smiling.

"Thanks," she said, stepping into the bathroom. The bolt was engaged.

She eyed herself in the mirror. She'd looked better, she thought. Much, much better, but at a time she couldn't remember. Her eyes were sunken, her cheeks shrivelled. Samantha could see her young, pretty self hidden behind the temporary hideousness.

Stripping, she stepped into the shower and let the hot rays pummel her for the next ten minutes. It was the first *hot* shower she'd taken in an age. After enjoying the heat of the water, she used the shampoo provided on the shower rack. She vigorously scrubbed her hair, giving it three washes. She was shocked at how much filth came out of her hair, which now shone black.

Grime slid down her gaunt body as she washed and rubbed at herself with a bar of soap. The drain clogged at one point, due to her dead hair catching in the plughole. Before she knew it, Sam was standing ankle deep in black, dirty water.

It almost brought tears to her eyes.

Oh, how she had let herself go, and it was all that fucking bitch's fault.

Samantha beat her fist against the shower wall, screaming, "You're fucking dead! Dead, dead, dead!" Water found its way into her mouth and was spat back out. When she'd finished hammering her fist, the bar of soap in her hand was reduced to nothing more than a lump of mush.

Switching off the water, and feeling a thousand times better, she dried, dressed, and picked up the rest of her things. Before leaving the bathroom, Samantha looked herself over in the mirror. She was pleased to see some colour back in her face. She was also happy with the clothes that had been selected for her.

Leaving the room, she was eager to be on the move again. She wanted to meet this Wadsworth fella, who would lead her to her sister. Sam couldn't wait to do Crystal in. If in fact the letter was no hoax, and so far, she had no reason to believe it was. Not after everything that had happened up to this point.

Hob was back behind his counter. He had a holdall of sorts in front of him.

"Here, I got you this," he said, brushing the dust off it. "I didn't want to see you putting that pretty dress of yours in a plastic bag, along with your money."

"And you definitely don't know who is doing all this?"

He had a sad expression on his face. "I swear to you, I don't. You look lovely, by the way."

She caught him looking at her perky tits – her nipples were pushing at the skin-tight fabric. "That's sweet of you," she said, walking up to the counter and putting her things into the bag Hob was holding open for her. "How far to the nearest bus stop?"

"It's about half a mile down the road. I'd be happy to—"

"No, it's fine. I need the fresh air, plus the walk will do me good," she interjected.

"Oh, okay," he said, sounding hurt.

Ten minutes later, he watched the way her arse moved beneath her equally tight jeans as she headed out the door.

"I bet the other two won't be as pretty as her," he muttered as he stood and waited for his second guest of the morning.

MEANWHILE, ALLIANCES ARE BEING MADE...

Crystal hadn't planned on staying. She'd just wanted to say hello to Mr. Tickles and tell him how awesome she thought his show had been. But then she'd recognised him as one of her inspirational figures from her childhood.

She also remembered his appearance in that book Harry found: *White Walls and Straitjackets*. A coincidence? Somehow, she didn't think so, what with the letter too. The weirdness was starting again, but she wasn't going to let on. Not yet.

Firstly, she was going to try and get as much information from Mr. Tickles as possible, without him getting angry.

Mr. Sugar Giggles had been a notoriously bad clown who travelled with *The Last Freak Show on Earth,* until he'd suddenly disappeared, never to be heard of or seen again.

Until now.

Crystal could hardly believe she'd run into him after so many years. She hadn't thought about him and his act in a long time. She'd always presumed him dead. He still looked as old as he did back then. It was eerie, she thought.

After their initial standoff in the big top, and her announcing that she was possibly his worst nightmare, Mr. Tickles had buckled. He'd smiled and offered her back to his tent, which was situated at the rear of the fairground. He shared his abode with Miss Sideshow Necrotic.

It wasn't much of a living space at that: It was dark, dank and stank of piss, shit and staleness. They shared their accommodation with a few of the circus ponies and Mr. Tickles' crow, Custard, who had been taught to speak a handful of vile words. On seeing Crystal, the bird had remarked how great her "bangers" were. She smiled, and thought of Harry and his foul mouth.

They'd get on like a house on fire! she thought.

Bales of hay also graced their home, which made for seating, along with a single bunk bed that was Mr. Tickles'. A bed made of loose hay served as Miss Sideshow Necrotic's place of rest. There was a bowl of water on the floor for her to lap at. Crystal also noted that there were a few bones skinned of their meat close to the bowl.

These are the real deal, Crystal thought. They're horrors on and off stage. But it didn't faze her. Nothing like keeping in character, I suppose. She then tittered to herself.

"Something amusing?" Mr. Tickles asked. Miss Sideshow Necrotic had crawled off into the darkness. Possibly onto her bed, Crystal thought. The chain leading from around her throat to Mr. Tickles' hand was almost taut.

"No, I was just thinking."

He bent over and wrapped the chain around a peg jutting out of the hay-scattered floor. He then sat before his mirror, which stood on top of an old broken-down desk. His 'chair' was an old milk crate. "Good. Sit down," he demanded, and with that, pulled out a full bottle of whiskey from one of the drawers, along with two glasses. Mr. Tickles ripped the cork from the bottle by using his sharp teeth, and spat it across the tent.

"Won't you need that?" Crystal asked.

"Don't get fucking smart with me! Besides, you ain't leaving here until this bottle's empty."

"But…"

"Once the cork's out, the bottle gets fucking drained, ya hear me?!" he asked. His lips pulled back over his teeth. His eyes were nothing more than dark sockets in the poor lighting.

He was fucking scary, she thought, but ultra cool at the same time. "Fine by me, I'm not some little girl."

"Oh, I can see that," he said.

Crystal smiled. "Why—" she was about to retort, but a sound caught her attention. Then a voice broke the near silence.

"A new plaything for me, Master Tickles?!" The tone was silky-smooth.

Mr. Tickles snorted a laugh. "Would you like that, Nightshade?" he asked.

Crystal turned this way and that on her seat. She couldn't tell where the third voice was coming from. "Who's that?" she asked the clown.

"Why, that's Miss Sideshow Nightshade," he said.

Necrotic giggled and clapped her hands together.

"Where is she?" Crystal asked.

"Why, behind you, dear!" Mr. Tickles said, pointing a finger over her shoulder. The nail was sharp, pointed

53

and black, much like his others. "Go and see her, if you dare…" he said before bellowing a laugh.

Rising off her seat, Crystal turned around and headed to the back of the tent.

"Watch your fingers…" Necrotic said before giggling.

"Yes, keep your hands away from the cage," Mr. Tickles warned.

Crystal stifled a laugh – they were good, fair play. She was a little rattled by it all as she pushed though the gloom. Nightshade's cage came into view, with the woman standing close to the bars. She was a lot smaller than Crystal had thought she would be.

"I'm the last vampire in the world," she said, smiling. She then extended her hand through the bars for Crystal to shake.

"I'd rather not," Crystal said, not getting too close.

"Suit yourself."

"You're such a dark-skinned beauty," Crystal remarked.

"My Harry would like you!"

"Who is Harry?" the vampirette asked.

"It doesn't matter," Crystal said, eyeing the girl. "What's your name?"

"Parris. I am American descendant."

"Why are you here?"

"I've roamed the earth for many, many years. Hundreds of years."

"Huh," Crystal huffed, "you don't look much older than twenty!"

"Ah, that's because a vampire never ages, my dear."

Crystal eyed the girl. In the half-light cast by a single lantern, she could see the girl sported dreadlocks. Not long ones, but short ones. She was wearing a tight, waist-high leather jacket, which had band patches scattered about it – Crystal caught sight of a Slipknot one, among many others. Her skin and teeth looked immaculate. They gleamed, considering her living conditions, Crystal marvelled. A few bones were scattered amidst rags on the floor about her.

"Cool footwear," Crystal commented, seeing that the girl was wearing odd-matching Converse.

"Thanks," Parris said, smiling anew.

And that's when Crystal saw the girl's sharp, pointed teeth. Crystal didn't know if it was the lighting or not, but Parris' eyes seemed to turn from a natural brown to an emerald green. She found it hypnotic.

"That's enough!" Mr. Tickles barked.

Parris broke her stare with Crystal. She whispered, "Maybe I'll get to play with you soon?!" Turning her back, she walked to the rear of her cage again.

"Come here, Crystal," he said as he poured the whiskey into the glasses in a slapdash way. He handed a tumbler to her. "Drink," he insisted.

She took a swallow.

Miss Sideshow Necrotic sniggered in the darkness as she uttered inaudibly to herself.

"Who is she?" she asked.

"Why, my faithful assistant. Just another freak in our wonderful circus," he said.

"I know that," Crystal said, taking another swallow. "But who *is* she?"

"She's been with me for a year now. I picked her up on the side of the road when the circus was heading into France."

"And her?" Crystal asked, pointing in Necrotic's direction.

"She was a mere child, sixteen, maybe seventeen, when I picked her up in Barry. She was cold, hungry and homeless."

"You took her in? Gave her a job?"

"I guess you could say that," he said, his teeth exposed once again. "She was walking around stark naked – she'd been beaten black and blue. Her cunt was running red. I assumed she'd had the shit raped out of her." He paused and licked his lips as though savouring the memory. "All she was wearing was a single shoe, which was a heel. Her sparkly dress and fancy underwear were strewn across the road – her bra was found in a bush close by." Again, he licked his lips. "After ten months, she finally spoke to me. Confided in me. She told me all that had happened to her. That four of them had followed her home from the pub and attacked her."

"Jesus," Crystal murmured. "She doesn't mind being chained like this?"

Mr. Tickles leaned forward, his breath reeking as he exhaled heavily in Crystal's direction. "Let's just say it's kind of strange how she loves it so much. She gets off on it." He smiled. "Another?" he asked, indicating Crystal's empty glass.

"Yes, please."

"Enough about me. How about you? What's your story?"

"Oh, I—" she started, but stopped herself. Do I mention *White Walls and Straitjackets*? she thought. Not yet.

"Everyone has a story," he said, pouring them fresh ones.

She sighed. "I'm a performer myself. I moved to Porthcawl about a month back." After taking a big swallow from her glass, Crystal could now feel the effects from the first drink, along with what she'd consumed with Harry earlier.

"Why here?" he asked.

"Why not? Here is as good as anywhere else."

"Hmm," he said, shrugging his shoulders. "Go on."

"We wanted to get away from the Valleys. Actually, we *needed* to get away, to make a fresh start with a new audience. The plan is to build up some cash, then maybe move on to London."

"I see. And who's *we?*"

"Oh, me and Harry – my partner. It's our show," she said, her smile faltering.

"What is it you do? What's your show about?" He took a big gulp from his untouched drink, almost draining it in one.

She too took a swig. "It's a ventriloquist act."

He smiled.

Miss Necrotic giggled in the darkness. "'*It's a ventriloquist act*.,'" she mocked.

Crystal shot a look in the woman's direction but couldn't see her target due to the gloom.

"Don't mind her," he said, stamping on the half-taut chain that belonged to his sidekick.

Crystal heard the woman choke and splutter, which brought a smile to her face. She'd love to strangle the bitch for real. Feel her pulse go weak under her grip as her tongue and head flopped.

Her knickers dampened with the thought as she took another slug of whiskey.

"Then Harry is your…doll?" he asked. The question had no cynicism or mocking to it.

She nodded, finished the whiskey, and asked for a third.

"My, my, you do like a tipple," he said, smacking his knee and stamping one big shoe on the ground. "*Beep-beep*," he then yelled at the top of his voice, sending Custard into a flapping, squawking frenzy.

"*Hoot-hoot*," Miss Sideshow Necrotic joined in.

"Maybe we should add her to our ever-growing freak show!" Parris said.

Crystal laughed. She couldn't remember the last time she'd felt so good, so serene about things, even though thoughts of the letter, her sister and the weird book were still at the back of her mind – was it all connected?

Her mind raced, which she put down to the whiskey kicking in.

Mr. Tickles freshened both glasses, giving hearty measures. His singles were quads, Crystal thought, eyeing the golden fluid. The big clown looked at the near empty bottle.

"Yes, Harry's my doll," she said.

"I'd like to meet him. To see your show," he said.

"You could come to the Pavilion one night? I'd like that. I've seen you so many times in the past."

"I very rarely leave the circus, my dear. I don't have the clothes or the personality to be among *your* society."

"What happens to the children from your show?" she blurted.

His smile faded. Miss Sideshow Necrotic fell silent. So did Custard.

"Tell her!" Parris said. "Tell her about my feasts!"

She gulped as Mr. Tickles arose from his seat and towered over her.

"Sorry," she back-pedalled, "I didn't mean to pry."

"If I told you," he said, his face darkened by the shadows of the dim light, drab clown make-up barely visible, "then I would have to kill you!" His eyes were completely hidden. His voice was low and growl-like. It reminded Crystal of a cornered animal – the type of noise it would make when confronted by an enemy of the wild.

The only things that broke the sudden silence were the low rattles of Miss Sideshow Necrotic's chain and the overhead lantern, which squeaked on its hook as it swung in the gentle breeze.

Crystal refused to shrink away from him this time.

He howled out a laugh then finished the last of his whiskey before hurling the tumbler out the tent. He got right into her face and breathed out a "*HAHAHA*!" She couldn't help but smile at his crazed ways.

"I'm just teasing you," he said. "I wouldn't kill a butterfly such as yourself," he said, stroking her face. His hand was dead cold. "The children fall through a trapdoor in the middle of the tent and are fed to my pet alligator. If they survive the pit, Parris gets to eat."

From her distance, Crystal could see the bloodstains on his pine, needle-like teeth. He was truly the most frightening person she had ever come across. But she was determined to keep her fears under wraps.

"Don't tell me your fucking lies!" she said, laughing.

Mr. Tickles unbent and looked up at Custard. "She doesn't believe us, Custard! Just as well," he said, joining in with Crystal as she laughed.

She wiped the rolling tears from her cheeks and spoke. "But seriously, I'd love for you to come and see Harry and me. I think you'd get on with him."

His smile died as his features took on a more sombre look. "I told you. I hardly leave the circus."

"But why?"

"For fear that the authorities will catch up with me."

Her insides went cold. "What did you do?"

"It was a long time ago. Before I became Mr. Tickles. Mr. Tickles was evil, and he lived inside my head. He wanted out, and so he did. I *became* him."

She said nothing, just waited for him to continue his story as she sipped at her drink.

"When he first started trying to get out of me, I was with *The Last Freak Show on Earth*, as you recall. I'd run away from home to join up when I was a child no more than twelve. I found my calling as the infamous clown Mr. Sugar Giggles. Some say the act was getting to me. Warping me. But no, Mr. Tickles had always been there, lying dormant. Biding his time. Mr. Sugar Giggles was a pussy – a pussy who needed phasing out.

"When my old ringmaster started seeing little changes in me, he got worried. Started keeping his eye on me. He got too close, and so I ended his life. This was before Mr. Tickles had fully come to the surface.

"They sent me down for it. Put me in this fancy asylum in—"

"Castell Hirwaun," Crystal said, finishing Mr. Tickles' sentence for him.

"How—"

"I have a sister there. But she escaped, and I think she's heading here to kill me and Harry. There's a party I'm supposed to be attending tonight, at—"

"379 Eagle Moss Av," he said, finishing her sentence in return.

The glass slipped from her hand as she looked up at Mr. Tickles. He was holding a letter which was identical to the one she had received earlier that evening. "Holy shit," she said. "I...I..."

"Had one as well?" he asked.

She nodded. "What does yours say?"

"Here, read it for yourself," he said, handing it to her.

Dear Mr. Tickles,

Firstly, let me say how nice it is to see you performing after years of being out of the game. I used to be such a fan of Mr. Sugar Giggles. Well, as the saying goes, you can't keep a good clown down!

My name is Wadsworth. You don't know me, as we have never met. But I know all about you. I appreciate your work and I know one of my other guests this evening will appreciate you too, as she also likes to perform.

That's right, I'm inviting you to a party – a get-together for…likeminded people. There will be some very, very interesting people here, one of which you will be most thrilled to meet!

Please do come along, as it will be in your interests to do so. Tomorrow evening at 20.00 hours. The address is 379 Eagle Moss Av, Porthcawl.

Also, bring Miss Sideshow Necrotic with you. It'll be a blast!

Yours sincerely,

Wadsworth

"I'm assuming he means you as the other performer?" Mr. Tickles said.

"What the hell is going on here?" Crystal snapped. "Are you in on this *shit*? Is Sam here?"

"Whoa, whoa. I'm just as in the dark as you. But I tell you one thing: I'm definitely going to attend that party. It's got my curiosity up, and I happen to think it has something to do with that book!" he said, pointing.

Her jaw dropped on seeing a copy of *White Walls and Straitjackets* on top of a box nearby. "You knew all about me, yet you quizzed me!"

He smiled. "As soon as I laid eyes on you, I knew who you were. Is it true about the murders?"

"You know what happened to the cat?" Crystal said.

"Yeah, and you know what satisfaction did! If it's good enough for a dead moggy, then it's good enough for Mr. Tickles."

She let a smile play across her face. "I think we all know the murders are true, don't we?"

"Yes, and that puts us in the same boat. Should the four of us attend this party together?"

"I'm not sure I'm going. I told you, my sister is in town, and my letter said she would be there. She'll try to take me out. Harry too."

Mr. Tickles arose from his crate, towering over her again. He displayed his teeth as he spoke. "Not with me around, she won't. I'll twist her head off like a chicken's and feed it to Nightshade. Be back here later this evening, and the four of us shall go together."

She laughed as she took a tumble over a few cases in the lobby, which had just been standing there. Her legs tangled with the luggage, which sent her headlong into a table holding a vase and a few other items. The objects were thrown to the air, only to smash against the ground.

Crystal was glad there was nobody about to see her stumbling around, pissed out of her head. She giggled on her way up the stairs as she bounded from wall to wall, trying desperately to dig her room key out of her jacket pocket.

Finally, she managed to free her key just as she tripped over the last step on the top flight of stairs. This caused her to crash against a door that was not hers. Rolling away from it, she staggered down the hall in search of her room, using the wall as support.

The EXIT sign, which hung from the ceiling and glowed green, emitted a slight buzzing sound. The annoying whistle scratched at her intoxicated brain. Picked at it like some sort of annoying little tic that was thirsty for blood.

Her head swam as she fumbled with the single key with a gigantic wooden fob attached to it. Three-hundred-and-thirteen was written on the oak block.

Trying to get the metal in its snug slot was a task on its own: Crystal jabbed and scuffed the door's varnished finish in her desperate attempts. "Fuck sake," she muttered, and tapped on the door. "Harry, are you awake? Let me in, will you!"

Putting her ear flush to the entry, she listened intently. Nothing came from the other side.

"Shit, he's probably still passed out. Hic-hic." She burped and collapsed against the wall.

"Excuse me, young lady, but people are trying to sleep around here, you know. We didn't pay good money to hear your rabblerousing ways at all hours!"

Crystal homed in on the voice, which was coming from up the corridor. Not quite a neighbour, but close. The man was rather tall, and wore glasses. He had on white boxer shorts and a vest to match. He wasn't skinny, nor was he fat.

He had a pretty face, Crystal thought. But that could have been the whiskey playing tricks on her. She stumbled over to him. The man's partner stood behind him, instructing him to "*tick*" her off.

Who the fuck uses a word like that?! Crystal thought. Lordy bastards.

They stood toe-to-toe and eye-to-eye in his doorway, except she was wobbling on unsteady legs whereas he was as solid as a concrete pillar.

"I shall be forced to call the management if this absurd behaviour continues," he said, his face getting redder and redder – speckles of sweat glistened on his upper lip and cheeks. "Do you know what bloody time it is?"

"Yes," the woman chirped. "It's bloody ludicrous. Harry and I pay good money to stay here every year, and not once have we had this kind of problem. Well, it's the Hilton next year," she huffed. "This place has lost its *appeal*."

Crystal laughed in the man's face. "Your name is *Harry*?" she asked, bursting with laughter.

"I don't see how this is at all funny. Gloria," he addressed his female companion. "Call them downstairs, this—" He gasped as Crystal's hand cupped his bollocks and squeezed. His knees buckled.

"Listen, punk," she maliciously whispered down his ear. "Tell that bitch of yours to get back to bed and to forget all this shit. Otherwise, I'll tear these off!"

"G…G…Gloria," he panted. "Just go back…*aarggghhh*…back to b-bed, dear." Now the sweat was in his eyes, forcing him to blink rapidly.

"Whatever is the matter…?" Gloria half shrieked when she saw what Crystal was doing. "You dreadful woman!" she spat. "Let my husband's…*husband* go!"

Crystal twisted the man's privates. "I'll rip 'em off!"

"*Please*, Gloria…" he said, now standing on tiptoes. "*Gooo* back to bed!" he wavered.

Crystal heard Gloria stomp off in retreat, and so she let her grip go. "I don't want to be hearing about any of this from the manager. Or I'll come back and finish the job," she said, pointing at his nuts.

"No, no, you won't have trouble, I promise," he whined. "Please."

"Good," she said, giving his left cheek a couple of soft slaps before walking away. She could hear Gloria ask Harry if his "bits" were okay and then offer to ice them for him. Crystal smiled, unlocked her door with the first attempt, and fell through the doorway. She landed on the floor with a thud, and then kicked her door shut from where she lay.

"Get the fuck up, you drunken bitch!" a voice inside the room said. "Where the fucking hell have you been? Been fucking some stranger out there on the slummy streets, have you? Get some good cock, did ya?"

She could feel *her* Harry pull at her hair roughly. "*Ahh*! Harry, please. You're hurting me!"

"I'll give you hurt, slut," he said, forcing his small hand into her mouth and grabbing her tongue. He repeatedly yanked, forcing tears from Crystal's eyes as she tried to speak. "Who was it?! *Who*!" he demanded. He slapped her once, twice, three times across the face before pulling her hair again. This time she was forced to crawl along the floor like a dog. "Move, tart. Move. *Now*!"

"Please, Harry. I lost track of time. I bumped into a friend. We had—"

Another hard slap crashed across her face – this one split her lip. Blood dribbled and dripped from her mouth and onto the carpet.

"I told you before what would happen if you ever fucked another behind my back."

Crystal's hands automatically went from her head and pressed against her pussy. "No, Harry, you wouldn't! I've done nothing wrong! Please, just listen to me."

She heard her butcher knife hit the floor, totally forgetting she still had the heavy weapon on her person. Harry heard it too, sending him into a deeper frenzy.

"Planning on fucking stabbing me as I slept, hey? You fucking callous slapper. I'll dig your insides out with it."

She felt sick from pain and drink, and, with that thought, spewed onto the carpet as she doggie walked along it.

"*Ugh*, you mucky pup," Harry said.

Finally, he let go of her hair and ordered her to get onto the bed. She did so, flopping onto it. The ceiling spun as Harry's voice echoed inside her head – it felt like someone was playing steel drums in there, with visions of sun-kissed beaches in Jamaica coming to mind. She stifled a laugh.

"Get your fucking clothes off!" Harry commanded.

She fumbled, not really knowing what the hell she was doing or what was going on. She couldn't remember the last time she was this out of her mind with alcohol. Her jeans were roughly tugged down; so too were her damp panties.

"And your fucking T-shirt."

She pulled that off, with Harry aiding her. Her clothes were scattered about the room as though they had exploded off her. He tore her bra from her body with such force that she heard the bone snap. That too was flung to one side, discarded like unwanted rubbish.

"Harry, please! Don't hurt me. I can explain what—"

"It's okay, bitch, I ain't going to hurt you. Why would I want to hurt such a fine creature?" he asked.

Harry's naked form was disjointed. Fuzzy. She forced her heavy eyes open, fearing he was going to cut her, because now he was holding the knife. She felt the cool steel tip scratch its way between her large tits, then circle each nipple. They stood erect, and she had to fight the urge not to put her hand between her legs and tease her own clit with her fingers.

"You like that, don't you?"

"*Mmm*," she groaned. "Yes, I do."

She bit her bottom lip hard as Harry continued to taunt her flesh with the butcher knife. He moved the blade from her breasts to her throat, and she felt the serrated edge sink slightly into her skin. She squealed, more with delight than fright.

Now her hand *was* between her legs, and her fingers eagerly stroked her G-spot. Harry laughed. His breath reeked of cigars.

Then the knife ran the length of her long, curved legs before he turned sharply and flung the knife in the door's direction. It bounded off the wood and skidded to a halt on the floor close to Crystal's bra.

He then pushed the hand she had buried between her legs to one side and inserted something into her. He probed her; it slipped in and out, taking her on a rollercoaster ride of sexual sensations. And then it was gone from her, whatever it had been.

Harry's rough, wooden mouth fused with hers, and soon his little hands were all over her tits.

The room had stopped spinning, but Crystal still felt nauseous. She was too horny to care as Harry turned her onto her side and spooned with her.

Then he was in her, ramming her time and time again, bringing her to a screaming climax as she came over and over again, much to Harry's grunting approval.

When they were finished, they both lay there, spent. Then Crystal drifted off into a dreamy, intoxicated sleep filled with knives and clowns and Harry and fucking and Samantha and dinner parties with strange butlers and her parents and dead children and alligators and circuses and candyfloss and vampires…

The slight parting in the curtains let the sun in. It was bright and stinging, bringing Crystal around in a cacophony of *"ugh"s, "ooo"s and "ahhh"s*. She rolled onto her back, a headache kicking in. She felt like shit – trodden in shit, which had been scraped up and dumped into a bin.

Her hair was a corkscrewed mess of knots and tangles, her make-up smudged and smeared all over her face and pillow. She kicked the covers off and let the sun massage its heat into her aching bones. She kept her eyes closed and nursed her sore head with one hand.

"How much did I bloody drink last night?" she asked aloud, before realizing Harry was in the room somewhere and that she still hadn't explained to him what had happened last night.

Cautiously, she opened her eyes and flicked her gaze around the room. He wasn't next to her. She thought he would have been because he'd fucked her and fallen asleep by her side. Or had he?

Then she found him, lying in one of the chairs by the window. The screech of gulls and roiling, smashing, crashing waves filtered into the room.

"Harry, are you awake?" Nothing. He didn't answer or look in her direction. He was either still very mad with her or sound asleep. "Harry?" she tried again. Nothing.

Crystal closed her eyes and thought about her tortured sleep before moving on to Mr. Tickles. She finally settled her mind on the patchy memory of her drunken fumble with Harry. It moistened her.

She wanted to play with herself, but refrained. She had lots to do before the party tonight, and she was still unsure on whether to go or not.

Rolling onto her side, Crystal kicked her legs over the edge of the bed and placed her feet on the floor. Her headache was starting to fade. She needed a mug of tea and a hot shower. She looked at her clothes, which were scattered about the room, haphazardly tossed by Harry.

Then she cast her eyes on the sex toy that lay among the garments. It was her dildo, its black exterior soiled with stale juices. She smiled. So that's what he was ramming in me, hey? she thought. Dirty bastard.

She stood and her head began to pound. As quickly as she could, Crystal staggered into the bathroom and locked the door. After starting the shower, she looked at herself in the mirror – her pretty face was hidden under her mucky, cabaret camouflage.

After removing the smudged make-up, she got into the shower and washed her hair and body before standing under the spray for at least five minutes. She let the warm water soak into her.

Getting out, she wrapped her long, dark hair in a towel before tying a second, larger one around her dripping body. She then stepped out of the bedroom. Harry was sat in the chair by the window.

"So, are you going to let me in on what you got up to last night, girl?" he uttered. His tone was cold. "Or am I going to have to hurt you for real this time?" And that's when she noticed the knife in his hand, which he'd taken off the floor.

"Don't be silly, Harry. Of course I'll tell you."

"Don't get lippy with me or I'll cut your lips off – both sets of them!"

"I just went for a walk along the front to try and clear my head – you won't believe how ugly it is on the streets here after dark, Harry. Gypos and carnies all over the fucking place. Not to mention leering pervs."

"Tell me more about the perverts. Did they harass you?"

"*Tut*, knock it off, Harry. I had the knife with me," she said, indicating with a nod of her head. "I wouldn't have taken much shit."

"What the fuck were you doing carrying such hardware, you stupid bitch?"

"Calm down, Harry. I took it just in case I bumped into Samantha. I would have taken her out if I had seen her, and that's a fact."

"If it was only a fucking 'walk' you went for, why in the fuck didn't you get in until the early hours? Why were you so pissed?!"

"Because I bumped into someone. This is what I was trying to tell you last night, before you went off on one. I met someone very, very interesting last night, and you're going to love him and his female assistants!"

Harry's eyes seemed to sparkle at the mention of 'female'. "Go on." His tone had now softened.

"His name is Mr. Tickles, and he's a clown with the circus that rolled in to town the other day. The females, Miss Sideshow Necrotic and Miss Sideshow Nightshade, are his sidekicks. They run this dark and murderous show. They're really fucked up, Harry!"

"Hmm, sounds interesting. What else?"

"Well, there are some very strange things going on around here, because I know this clown from years back. From when I was a little girl." Crystal then proceeded to tell Harry about why Mr. Tickles had changed his identity.

"Sounds like our sort of man!"

"Not only that, Harry, but he too has received a letter from this Wadsworth fella, telling him that he has also been invited to the 'party', along with his partner, Miss Sideshow Necrotic. I told him all about my fears of going and about Samantha, blah, blah, blah, and he offered for us all to go together."

"What in the fuck is going on?" Harry mused, seemingly talking to himself and not Crystal.

"I think we need to go, Harry."

"We'll possibly have to kill your sister, and maybe others!" Harry said.

"Then so be it, Harry."

"That's what I like to hear, slut."

"I told Mr. Tickles we'd be at his tent by seven."

"Good."

"There's one other thing, too…" she said.

"What?"

"He's the clown from the book, Harry. That *White Walls* book…"

Harry's jaw dropped. "Are you sure?" he whispered.

Crystal nodded. "We need to find out what the fuck is going on, Harry."

"Don't worry. I'm sure we'll get all the answers we're looking for tonight."

"Uh-huh," she said. "Being as we are not working today, why don't we have a bit of what we had last night this morning?" she asked, letting her towel drop to the floor before giving him a cheeky wink.

THE SECOND VISIT...

He didn't want to leave his cell. He was safe here, and women were safe on the outside with him in here. Also, he was making progress with his doctor and in his therapy groups. She'd even said that to him herself.

"Norm, I think we are making real progress. You've finally come to terms with the fact that your wife, Angharad, is dead, and that it wasn't really her telling you what to do. That it was all in your head."

Progress. That's a good word, he thought.

That word was Norm Jenkins' safety blanket. He clung to it much like a three-year-old clings to a blanky, which, in return, had helped him through his darkest days at the hospital.

Through the progress had come reward. Through reward had come more progress, until they'd moved Norm from maximum to medium security. In time, if he continued to progress and show willing, he would be moved to minimum security. But first, his doctor had to know he was no longer a threat to himself or others.

If he had to wait, then he would. For now, Norm was happy. He had the pleasure of a cosy room instead of a cell, with no bars or locks, and he could come and go as he pleased. He wasn't caged like an animal any longer, and for that, he was grateful. Probably happy enough to see out his days in this part of the hospital – he didn't really require minimum security.

He just didn't want to hurt anyone. Not ever again.

But then the note had come.

And just like that, he could almost feel the regression kick in.

Having come back to his room from a game of chess with one of the other patients, Norm had found a small, stuffed package on his pillow. Intrigued, he went to it excitedly and tore the envelope open in one vicious pull. A wire, along with a large key, fell to the bed and puzzled him, until he found the accompanying letter. It was slightly ruffled by his eagerness.

He made sure no one was around. With the coast clear, he began to read, hoping to make some sense of it all.

Dear Norm,

Angharad is waiting...

That first line made his breath lodge in his throat. He fell against the wall as a wave of nausea and dizziness kicked in. His knees felt weak and his brow broke into a flood of sweat.

Giving himself five minutes to recover, Norm took to his bed and sat on its edge. There was a glass half full of water on his bedside table. He swallowed the lot in one go, not caring about the tracks that dribbled out of his mouth and down his chin, spattering the letter he held in his shaking hand. The paper rustled.

Panting, he closed his eyes and counted to ten, which helped calm his inner self, breathing and heart rate.

He opened his eyes. The letter was still there. He was glad of that, fearing the hallucinations may have been coming back. The paper was real. The words were real.

Angharad is waiting...

He turned his gaze away from the offending words, about to call for the nurse housed in her little station just down the hall. But something stopped him. Her name, that's what it was. *Angharad.* It stirred in him something unstoppable. All consuming. His heart began to pound, but he managed to slow it by doing his breathing exercises.

"Breathe, Norm, that's it. One...two...one...two..." he said aloud. "One...two...one...two." Feeling better, he lifted the letter and reread the offending line.

Angharad is waiting...

So too am I...Along with a whole host of other guests at my home – 379 Eagle Moss Av, Porthcawl.

I'd like you to join us, as would your delightful wife. She tells me she is missing you deeply. Surely you wouldn't want to disappoint her?

Take the wire from the parcel and kill the male guard that walks the corridors outside your door at night. Make sure you make your move at midnight. Also, take the key, as it is a skeleton key and will open every locked door between you and the outside.

When the guard is dead, take his clothes and make your escape. By this time, all hell should have broken loose inside the hospital, which will make your escape easier.

Once out, locate your pickup truck, which is awaiting you on the grounds. Once inside it, you'll find another letter. That one will give you further instructions on what to do.

Yours sincerely,

Wadsworth

Where the reforming Norm went to, he had no idea.

All he knew was that his wife was still out there, and she was waiting for him. It enraged him to think that these bastards here had told him she was dead.

The rage was like lava spilling out of an erupting volcano. Killing a single guard to be reunited with his Angharad was a small price to pay. Especially after everything he had done for her.

He hid the letter, key and wire under his pillow and climbed under the sheets. Clive, the guard who always worked the late shift, would be in to check on him at around ten for lights out. He could strike then, but the letter told him he should wait until midnight because *"all hell should have broken loose inside the hospital"* by then.

He wasn't really sure what that meant, but if Angharad was behind his escape, then he fully trusted her…

At precisely ten o'clock, Clive came to Norm's room to wish him a good night. He then left to do the rest of his round. Norm had asked the ageing guard if he would mind popping back in on him from time to time, as he was having a restless time of it. Clive had been happy to oblige, which would be his ultimate downfall.

Just after midnight, when Clive returned to Norm for the third time, Norm was waiting behind his door, the wire taut between his hands.

The thin cord cut deep into the man's ageing flesh as Norm pulled as tight as he could. Clive choked and tried to pull the wire from around his throat, but it was all in vain, as his strength was no match for Norm's.

When Clive was finally dead, Norm took his clothes, shut his door and proceeded without a problem. As promised, he managed to pass through the corridor and doors with the key he had been provided with. No one seemed to notice him. Sirens wailed far off in the hospital as nurses and guards at their desks and front door let him stride by, causing him to laugh at the simplicity of it all.

Finding his pickup, which was unlocked, he got in. "Good old Angharad," he said. "She always thinks of everything." Smiling, he ripped the second envelope off the steering wheel and tore it open.

Dear Norm,

If you are reading this, then you have made it to the outside, untroubled, I hope, and are sat in your pickup. Inside the glove box you will find a map to a place called Hob's, which is a café on an old road close to Hirwaun.

You'll need to go inside the café and ask for the owner, Hob. He will be expecting you, and will provide you with everything you need: Food, clothes, money and a bus ticket, which will see you to Porthcawl. He will also give you a third and final letter. When we do meet, I can promise you that it will be more than worth your while. And, as promised, your lovely Angharad is waiting...You have my word.

Warmest,

Wadsworth

Balling the letter and tossing it onto the passenger's seat, Norm opened the glove compartment and took out the road map.

He couldn't remember the last time he'd held one. It was practically double-Dutch to him as he looked at the directions marked out in front of him. Thinking he'd grasped it, he started the engine, pulled off, and headed for Hob's café.

After losing his way countless of times, Norm finally pulled up outside the café at God knows what time. It was still dark, yet the whole of Hob's was lit up like a Christmas tree. He watched as a young, thin woman left the place with a bag over her shoulder. She appeared to be in a great hurry and was swallowed by shadows before Norm could get his cumbersome frame out of the van.

He had little fear walking up to the door of the café, because he knew Angharad was involved in all of this.

Walking through the door of Hob's, his ears picked up the sounds coming from the kitchen – something was being fried in a pan. Bacon or eggs, maybe even sausages. This told him he was indeed expected by the owner, who was probably cooking food for him, as the place was empty.

Walking towards the counter, Norm scanned the place with erratic eye movements. Should I call out? he thought. It might be a good idea. He stopped in his tracks, about to open his mouth, when a face popped out from behind a door that Norm assumed led to the kitchen.

The chubby face looked hot, flustered and not at all amused. Maybe even a bit anxious or weary. "Norm?" the man said.

Norm nodded.

"Norm Jenkins?"

How many other Norms are you expecting to drop by tonight, Norm wanted to say, but didn't. He just nodded and uttered, "Hob?"

"Yeah," the man said, stepping out of the kitchen. His large, wobbly frame filled the doorway.

Norm's gaze met the steel bat that the restaurateur held in one had whilst he lightly clubbed the other. "Are you going to be a good boy, Norm?"

Norm nodded and smiled. Hob reminded him of a fat Texan tycoon – all that was missing was a belt buckle complete with bull horns and a ten-gallon hat. "You don't have to worry about me. All I want is the food, clothes money and ticket you're supposed to provide me with. After that, I'll be on my way," Norm said in a calm tone.

"Go and grab a seat over there," Hob said, indicating with a dip of his head. "I've put your letter on the table. After you've eaten, I'll show you where you can shower and change before giving you the rest of your stuff."

"Okay," Norm said. "Have you seen my Angharad?"

"Who?" Hob said.

"My wife. It said in the first letter…"

"Look, like I told the one before you, I know nothing about what's going on, okay? Please, just do what you have to do and go. All I'm trying to do is run a business."

Norm eyed the man for a second, seeing and hearing the fear in him, before nodding and turning to head for his seat.

"Your food will be over in a mo. You want anything to drink?"

"What have you got?"

"We have hard stuff, if that's what you mean?"

"Just something soft. Maybe a juice. What are you cooking up? It smells lovely!" Norm said, taking his seat and picking up the third and last envelope.

"Full English."

"Lovely. I've not had one of them in a long time," Norm said, his mood cheery. He couldn't wait to see his beloved.

Sitting at the table, which had cutlery and condiments awaiting him along with the envelope, he drank the place in. The American theme amused him. He giggled, shook his head and picked up the letter. It felt thicker. Slightly heavier. On tearing it open, a photo fell from the neatly folded paper, which had a perfume aroma on it.

"*Angharad*," Norm whispered as he feverishly opened the letter and ignored the snapshot that lay picture-up on the table.

Dear Norm,

My love,

I hope this letter finds you well and safe at Hob's Café? I eagerly await you at the home of Wadsworth. He has been nothing but friendly towards me. Enclosed in this letter is a photo of me in the company of our host for this evening's gathering. Do hurry, Norm – I've missed you.

All my love,

Angharad

Norm held the sheet of paper close to his nose and deeply breathed in the sweet smelling perfume, which had been lovingly squirted over the letter. Tears slid down his face as he cast the letter to one side and looked at the photo. It depicted his beautiful wife in her wheelchair, and standing behind her was a well-groomed man, his face darkened by poor lighting. But that was Angharad. Definitely.

Hob's voice startled Norm from his hazy daydreams. "You okay, pal?"

Norm looked up at the café owner and wiped his tears away. "Yes," he said in a gentle manner.

"Right you are," Hob said, placing a plate in front of him. "A good old English for you, son. It'll help build your strength up."

Norm looked at the stodgy food before him. He wasn't normally a fan of fried foods, as he liked to look after himself, what with his previous job and everything. But he guessed that didn't matter much these days, and began to dig in, happy with the thought of seeing his woman once again. I won't mess it up this time, he thought. *Huh-uh.* No chance. He grinned as he chewed and tore at his food.

Hob turned and walked away, slightly chilled by Norm's behaviour. "I'll let you get on with it, pal. Just give us a shout when you're ready to get cleaned up."

"Will do," he said.

The vicious scraping of cutlery on plate set Hob's teeth on edge. His insides shivered. "Hurry up and get the fuck out," Hob said under his breath as he stepped back behind the counter and eyed Norm for a while. He watched as Norm grinned and spoke to himself.

Hob's hands found the shaft of Old Rosie, just to make sure she was still where he'd left her...

Fifty minutes later, Hob handed Norm a plastic bag filled with the dinner suit, watch, bus ticket and cash. The dishevelled man that had walked through Hob's door over an hour ago was gone, scrubbed away with the grime and sweat.

"Thanks," was all Norm said as he took the plastic bag from Hob.

"You'll find a bus stop down the road. I would drive you, but I can't leave the place..."

"It's okay," Norm interjected, turned, and left.

Hob felt relived as he watched the man go. He didn't take his eyes off Norm until he was out the door and out of sight. "Two down, one to go..."

THE FINAL VISIT…

He stood facing his cell door and waited with impeccable patience for it to be unlocked. The light inside his six-by-four room was out, along with the ones in the corridor.

The holding cells were much smaller in this part of the hospital, known as 'The Bowels.' They were tight and claustrophobic, and only the most dangerous and depraved were kept this far down. Some joked that the rooms were a hundred feet below surface, but Klaws knew that to be a lie – it was more like two hundred feet. That thought made him smile. "Like a rat in a tunnel…" he whispered.

Turning his head slightly, he looked at the crumpled letter on his bed. Whoever's doing this is being a very, very naughty child. They won't be getting any presents this Christmas. Uh-huh, he thought. It'll be a whipping to the death for that bad boy or girl.

But, as they lay dying, I'll thank them. Thank them for setting me free and returning my special, special keepsake. Opening his hand, he looked down at the earring with cutlass pendant. Again, he smiled. A low rumble filled his throat as he affixed the piece of jewellery to his ear.

Now all I need is my suit and boots, he thought.

That had been promised in his letter – that and other things he needed were awaiting him at a café called Hob's. Klaws knew the café owner and his wife. They were extremely naughty – had been for many years. Paying them a visit this evening would be most fitting, what with it being Christmas Eve, he thought.

With the earring attached, he gave it a flick and listened to it rattle before walking over to his bed and picking the letter up. He looked over it again. *"At precisely midnight, your cell door will be unlocked...I'll be waiting for you..."* He read, then reread the address to make sure it was Hob's he was heading to next.

"A limo will be waiting for you on the hospital grounds...It'll take you to where you need to go."

Crushing the letter into a ball, he threw it over his shoulder and listened to it bounce off the wall and land on the floor at his feet. He pounded his open right hand with his left fist. The sound of flesh striking flesh caused the hairs at the back of his neck to rise.

With his left first cupped by his right hand, he cracked his knuckles, then did the same to his right. Klaws then rotated his head and shoulders until the bones cracked and settled. He felt good and loose.

Excited energy caused him to start bouncing on his toes. He swayed from side to side like a boxer – for a large man, he had the nimbleness of a ballerina. As he moved about energetically, he started to recite *'Twas the Night Before Christmas*.

Before he could reach the end of Clement's beloved Christmas poem, Klaws heard keys rattle in the door's lock. He stopped talking and stood still. When he heard the bolts disengage, he moved forward – his hands were held up in front of him, ready to strike.

The door groaned as it was pushed open.

"You're free," a voice whispered into the room. All Klaws could see in the poor light was a dark, blobby form at best.

"My, my, what a naughty one you are. Trying to stay up to catch a glimpse of Santa, young one?" Klaws roared as he put his massive hands to the door and ripped it wide.

"*Huh*!" the freer gasped. A heavy jingle-jangle sound filled Klaws' ears, making him assume a bunch of keys had hit the deck. "No, please!" the man cried as Klaws grabbed the smaller bloke by his jacket. "I—" the person was about to plead again, but he was roughly pulled into the tiny room.

Klaws threw the man against the back wall, then jumped on him and crushed him to the floor. He then sank his teeth into the man's cheek and tore parts of it free. Before the captured man could scream, Klaws clamped a hand over his mouth, then spat the loose, bloody mess onto the floor.

"'Twas the night before Christmas…" he started, then forced his hand into the jailer's mouth and grabbed his tongue. With one fierce yank, the organ came flapping out – the squelching sounds delighted the deranged Santa as he spoke the merry, poetic words.

Sugar plums danced in his head.

As the man lay choking on his blood and vomit, Klaws made his way over to the open door. He licked his fingers clean before picking up the keys and heading out into the corridor.

Behind him, he could hear the vicious sobs of a pained soul.

"That's what naughty boys get," he said, making his way down the darkened passageway. Before starting his ascent to the higher floors, Klaws opened the doors to all the cells on his floor. "I can be naughty, too!" he said, sniggering. "Ho-ho-ho, Merry Christmas!" he bellowed before making his way up the steel steps.

He heard other prisoners shuffle out of their cages behind him – some whooped and cheered as they opened their doors to freedom. "Thanks, Santa!" one called. "That's just what I wanted for Christmas!" another yelled.

"My pleasure, children!" Klaws called back. "Just remember to be good *alllll* year round!"

On the second floor, which was still way below the surface, Klaws killed both guards and freed the prisoners housed there before making his way upward once again. When he approached the third floor, a heavy door barred his way, but that was of no problem – he still had the set of keys.

Once through that door, familiar sounds filled his ears, along with blaring sirens in the distance. Frantic distress calls for guards, nurses and doctors came flooding over the Tannoy speakers, which caused Klaws to giggle. "What an exciting Christmas Eve," he said, watching hospital personnel dash around in utter panic.

Looking up the long corridor, Klaws spotted a nurse being pinned to the floor by three escapees. As one held her, another ripped her uniform off. This left the third man to dispose of her shoes, tights and knickers.

"Ho-ho-ho!" Klaws cried. "Merry Christmas!" he concluded, before stalking off. When he came to another locked door, he used the keys once again. As he neared the main door, two armed guards pounced on him.

One of them managed to press a taser device to his back whilst the other started clubbing him with a baton.

They forced him to one knee before he managed to grab the arm holding the shock gun. He yanked and forced the one guard to taser his colleague, who yelped and collapsed to the floor. As he rolled around holding his guts, Klaws set on the other man.

"*Please!*" he had time to say before Klaws rammed the stun gun into the chubby man's mouth. Klaws triggered the gun, and the man's whole mouth lit-up. Smoke billowed out his nostrils and the air filled with a charred, fleshy smell.

When the man became floppy in his grip, he let the body hit the floor with a cataclysmic thud. Before leaving the building via the main entrance, Klaws stamped on the other guard's throat, thus crushing the man's windpipe, causing him to die within minutes.

Once outside, he stood in the night breeze for a full five minutes before moving on. It felt good to have the wind tousle his hair and lick his skin.

It wasn't hard to find the limo, which was parked in the visitor's car park. The car was huge, black and sleek. The moonlight radiated off the paintwork in a mesmerizing way. Where are my deer? he wondered.

Going to the driver's side of the limo, Klaws noticed the window glide down a crack. "Get in!" a voice demanded.

He didn't care for the arsehole's tone. He wanted nothing more than to punch a hole in the glass and break the driver's neck. But he knew he couldn't do that – he needed this person's help to get him to where he was supposed to go. Begrudgingly, he went to the back door and got in.

Klaws sat in silence as the car pulled away. Before him, on a shelf, was a line of alcohol bottles. Pulling a gin bottle free, he uncapped it and started downing the hard spirit. When the bottle was empty, he threw it to one side and grabbed the letter that was taped to a whiskey container. "Klaws" was written across the plain white envelope.

Pulling the letter free, he read it with disinterest. Finishing it, he crumpled it into a ball and threw it – it bounced off the screen which divided the front and back of the expensive car. "That fucker better know where he's going!" Klaws slurred. "I have a lot of presents to deliver this evening."

When the car broke hard, Santa Klaws woke up and wiped the drool out of his beard. "Where…where am I?!" he yelled, then became startled as the car's intercom burst to life.

"You've reached your destination. If you could kindly get out, that would be most appreciated!" the driver barked.

Through foggy eyes, Klaws looked out his window. He could see the café. All the lights appeared to be on inside, but there were no cars in the car park, apart from one. Probably Hob's, he thought.

"Get out!" the voice boomed over the intercom again.

This enraged Klaws, who sat up and put his fist through the glass divider. The driver shrieked as he was pulled back as far as his belt would allow. "Not nice, not nice, not nice!" Klaws repeated over and over again as he crushed the man's head between his enormous hands.

Bones crunched, and blood trickled out of the driver's ears and nose.

When he stopped thrashing, Klaws pushed the man away from him before getting out of the car. He closed the door with a heavy thud, which rocked the limo on its chassis. I'll take the car later, he thought.

Smiling, he stepped up to the door of the café.

A bell jingled as he entered.

When he saw the limo pull into the car park, Hob had felt slightly relieved because he knew this whole situation would be over and done within the next thirty or forty minutes. But when he saw the car rocking violently, an icy nest of vipers settled in his guts.

All was not well.

This was further stressed when Hob latched his sights on the man dubbed 'Santa Klaws' – his hands looked as though they had been dipped into a bucket of red paint. The crimson trails climbed his arms to his elbows, with patches of the stuff all over his hospital fatigues.

"He looks like a mountain!" Hob uttered, watching the man approach the door. He's that tall, Hob thought, that his trousers look like hot pants. The closer he got, Hob could see a line of bloody freckles across the bridge of the man's nose.

When the doorbell chimed, Hob came out of his trance and smiled. "You must be Santa?" he said, putting his hand out for the man to shake. When the offered hand was taken, Hob instantly regretted it. The blood was still fresh on the man's hand, which engulfed Hob's hand and left a sticky, gooey mess. The grip was vice-like, and Hob thought his bones would fold under the extreme pressure. "Nice to meet you!" he said between gritted teeth.

Klaws grunted in reply.

"Well, I'm sure you're eager to be on your way. There's a plate of food for you over there, along with a letter. Once you're done, I'll show you were you can get cleaned up."

This time, Klaws said nothing, just looked straight through Hob.

"If you'd like to sit down…" the café owner tried pushing.

But still Klaws didn't move, just continued to stare, unblinking.

Slowly, Hob backed away. His vision caught sight of Rosie. "I'll be in the back if you need me," he said, continuing to retreat.

The mist seemed to clear from Klaws' vision, and so he nodded before turning to go to his table.

A sigh escaped Hob. Thank God for that, he thought as he retreated into the kitchen. From there, he watched as the big man sat at one of his tables and grabbed the letter. He tore it open with such viciousness that Hob thought there would be nothing left, just confetti.

The contents of the letter didn't appear to grab his attention, as he looked at it briefly before throwing it to one side. Shaking is head, a smile spread across his face – this one's a right fucking weirdo, Hob thought.

But the smile was short-lived, as he watched Santa Klaws eat his food with his bare hands. He rammed bacon and sausages into his mouth like a wild animal. Once the meat was gone, he picked the plate up and angled it. He then let the beans slide off it and into his mouth. With the plate empty, he threw it against the wall.

This caused Hob to jump back. That's it, he thought. This freak is leaving now! Storming out of the kitchen, Hob grabbed Rosie and the rest of Santa Klaws' belongings. "I think it's time you were on your way, pal," he said, tossing the bag onto the table where Klaws sat.

He didn't move. He just stared at the bag in front of him.

"Hey, dickhead!" Hob said, jabbing the big man with the end of the clubbing instrument. "I said it's time to leave! Get up and start walking, pal. Everything you need is in that bag."

Still the man didn't move.

"Look, I've tried to be as decent as I can with you, but I'm starting to lose my rag!" Hob said, giving the man a few extra hard pokes in the arm with the bat. "You come in here, take my food, then start smashing my stuff – uh-huh, I'm not having it. Up!" Hob barked.

Santa turned his head to one side and looked up at Hob. A low growl formed in his throat. Slowly, he got up. Hob backed away.

"Don't come any closer!" the restaurateur said, fear evident in his tone. "I'm not afraid of taking you down," he threatened.

The jukebox kicked to life as Hob's back found it. He held the bat out in front of him. "Please, get back!" he shouted, swinging the sports instrument.

But this didn't stop Klaws. He caught a hold of the bat in mid-swipe and ripped it out of the café owner's hands. He then threw the bat to one side, grabbed Hob by his hair and shoulder, and then spun him in a circle.

"Hob, what's going on down there?!" a voice called.

"Bella! Help! Call the police!"

"*Hob*?!" Bella called back, her voice frantic.

Hob heard footfalls drawing closer to him.

"Don't come down here, Bella! Please, stay...*Aaaargh*!" Hob bellowed as his face was driven into the jukebox once, twice, three times. Glass exploded as the machine, along with Hob's head, was destroyed.

"Jesus! Hob!" Bella cried, which was followed by the sound of her rushing footfalls.

With Hob's head inside the player, he stayed upright – shards of glass held him in place. Blood pooled at his feet as it pissed out the bottom of his trouser legs.

Klaws couldn't help but watch the body until it stopped twitching. Like a fish on a hook, he thought, smiling.

It was only when the woman started to shriek that Klaws managed to break his gaze. Turning, he saw the fat woman run for the kitchen. He stalked after her and cornered her by the stove.

She had a cleaver in her fat, shaking paw. "You get the fuck away from me, or I'll cut you in two! *Bastard*!"

Klaws avoided the woman's pathetic attempt at slicing him open, as he grabbed her wrist and broke it. She yelped, but screamed when her elbow and shoulder both blew from his roughhousing.

"P...P...P..." she tried to speak between staggered sobs. "I...I...*Arrgh*!" she yelled when her ruptured arm was forced behind her back. She instinctively stood on her toes as she tried to pull away from the pain.

But he had her pinned like a bunny in a snare.

"No..." she pleaded on seeing Klaws lift a pot from off a lit hob. The water within the cooking utensil bubbled with heat. Piss ran down the inside of her legs and splashed the white tiles that helped make up the kitchen's pristine flooring.

All she had time to do was gasp as her face was drenched with scalding water. Bella could hardly thrash, either, as he had her squashed against the kitchen worktops. After a couple of seconds, Klaws tossed the pot to one side and threw the fat bitch across the kitchen.

Little of her face remained. The flesh had fallen away, dissolved. She screamed and screamed, but this did little to stop the wannabe Father Christmas, as he

grabbed a rolling pin off a worktop and took to her with it.

Blood spewed up the walls as he clubbed her about the face and body. He savagely grunted and growled as he put the work and effort in. After beating her to within an inch of her life, the dough pin snapped in two, forcing him to stop.

Enraged, he turned all the oven hobs on before scooping her up and throwing her down onto the naked flames. Bella didn't react, as she was practically dead.

As he walked out of the kitchen, he heard her go up with a *whooping* sound. Going back to where Hob 'stood', Klaws picked up the baseball bat and his bag from off the table.

By the time he reached the limo, Hob's Café was engulfed in flames and black smoke. The windows blew outwards, casting the car park in tiny shards of glass.

Klaws smiled as he opened the door and pulled the driver out. I'll just leave the cunt here! he decided. Getting behind the wheel, he threw the bat and bag onto the seat beside him. He didn't have time to look through things just yet – he could already hear sirens in the distance.

By putting the limo into gear, Klaws pulled away from the crumbling café. He smiled as he looked in the rear-view mirror and saw sections of it fall to the ground.

"Ho-ho-ho! Merry Christmas," he said before turning the radio on.

THE FIRST ARRIVAL...

When the bus finally pulled into the depot at Porthcawl, Sam felt massively relieved. She hadn't expected such an unhampered journey, what with her escape from Castell Hirwaun.

Surely they know I'm gone by now? Where are the roadblocks? The armed guards?

Nothing.

The trip from Hirwuan had been peaceful. When she'd first got on the bus, nobody had occupied it apart from the driver. Having chosen the backseats, she'd lain down and drifted off into a peaceful, relaxing sleep – the nightmares, thankfully, had stayed away.

When she'd awoken, the bus had been leaving Bridgend, a town situated a few miles outside of Porthcawl. The sun had been high in the sky, with most of the seats on the bus filled.

She'd felt slightly silly, waking up with so many people looking at her. Drool had found its way into her hair, but she'd not wanted to clean it out with so many eyes on her. Thirty minutes after that, the bus had arrived at the seaside town, to which the driver announced, "If you're going farther, you'll need to change here, people!"

The morning sun was strong as she got off the bus. She couldn't remember the last time she had felt so free, so at peace. The sea air filled her nostrils as gulls swooped and squawked above her. *Whatever happens, I'm not going back*, she thought. *I'll die first. And that's more than likely going to be the outcome, if I'm going to be seeing Crystal later.*

If I go down, that bitch is coming with me!

As she walked away from the depot, Sam headed for the seafront. From there, she was able to get her bearings.

Passing a clock, she noticed it was only eight o'clock – *what am I going to do for the next twelve hours? I can't very well lug this stuff around all day*, she thought. *I could check in to a hotel? Whoever sent me those letters also supplied me with cash. I could use it to get a room. I wasn't told any different.*

Once on the seafront, Sam looked about her. The streets were dead. The fairground was deserted. Apart from a few seagulls here and there, Sam was practically alone. Not many cars passed her, either. The place seemed like a ghost town. The thought made her shiver.

Pushing her thoughts to the back of her mind, Sam scanned the signposts and saw that the town of Porthcawl was to her left. Sam followed the directions and soon found herself in a small street crowded with shops, cafes and newsagents. Some had already opened for business, whilst other shops and windows remained dark.

Confused as to which way to go next, her eyes fell on a little coffee shop by the name of *Almond Croissant*, which was showing signs of life. *Hmm, I could sit and* have a coffee, she thought. I'm sure the owner or one of the staff members will know of a decent B&B or hotel.

Yes, good idea.

Moving quickly to the shop, Sam took a seat inside and waited for the young blonde waitress to come to her table. "A black coffee, please," Sam ordered. The young girl smiled and nodded before turning on her heel and heading for the kitchen.

Sam could hear coffee pots, cups and spoons rattling in the distance. A thick aroma of coffee clung to the air. In that moment, she felt normal. Well, as normal as normal can feel, she thought as she took in the quaint décor of the coffee shop.

Whimsical paintings of boats at sea dotted the walls, along with others depicting trawlers and such anchored at bays and harbours. Other portraits consisted of flowers and cottages, which were soothing to look at.

The paintings worked well with the calming colour schemes of the walls along with a flowery border. All the tablecloths, seatbacks and covers, placemats, cutlery and salt and pepper shakers matched – nothing seemed out of place.

As the staff prepped the drinks and food behind the scenes, they listened to a radio, which Sam could pick up on. The words and music were very faint over the sound of the general hustle and bustle of the working café.

"One coffee!" the waitress said, placing it in front of Sam. "Is there anything else I can get you? The sugar is here on the table."

"Oh, er…No, that will be all, thank you," Sam replied as she looked down at the coffee and complimentary biscuit, which was placed on the saucer next to the cup. Picking the offering up, Sam proceeded to open the foil packet which encased it. Before she put

the treat into her mouth, it suddenly dawned on her – there *was* something else.

"Erm, excuse me?" she called after the waitress.

"Yes?" the young girl said, turning to face Sam. For the first time, Sam noticed a tiny croissant emblem on her polo shirt – the words "Almond Croissant" were written above it in an arch.

"Could you tell me if there's a B&B close by?"

"Yes, there's one just around the corner. Cheap, too!"

"That's brilliant. Where can I find it?"

"If you take a left when you leave here, you'll see B&M at the bottom of the street – walk to that shop and take another left. The B&B will be there on your left. It's called The Anchor. You can't miss it," the waitress said, smiling.

"Thank you, you've been most helpful."

"No problem!"

When the waitress returned to the kitchen, Sam was once again left with her thoughts. As she slowly chewed her biscuit, she thought of Crystal. I wonder if she's here yet? The letter promised I'd come face-to-face with her tonight.

Finishing the biscuit, which tasted disgusting, Sam washed it down with the coffee. Enough time had passed for her to be able to drink it in one go. Now that she had a destination, she was keen to get moving again. Not only that, but the thought of having her own room for the day, with a bath, made her eager to go.

Getting up, she went to the counter to pay, then left. Once on the street again, Sam faced left and immediately saw the massive shop called B&M. It was hard to miss, what with its size and gaudy blue and orange colours decorating the front of the building. Nodding, she headed for it.

Once there, she took a left and walked down a short alleyway. Just when she thought she'd taken a wrong turn, or that the bitch back at the café had no idea what she was talking about, Sam came across the Anchor Hotel. It appeared to be attached to a pub with the same name.

"Okay, this looks nice," she said, walking through the main entrance.

When she came across the reception desk, she chimed the bell on the countertop.

"Coming!" a voice called from somewhere in the distance.

Sam put her bag down and looked about her. The place seemed very cheery, with its cream and white colour scheme. Little lights in the shapes of candles clung to the walls here and there. They sat in sconces, their bulbs bare. Not a spot of dust or dirt could be seen.

On the receptionist's countertop lay a decent amount of magazines and newspapers. Guest were encouraged to "Take *one* to their room" and so Sam picked up one of the magazines, which had last week's date on it. It doesn't matter, she thought. It'll be nice to see what's going on in the world!

"Hello!" a voice called, and a skinny, bespectacled man dashed through an opening at the back of the reception area. "Can I help?"

"Oh," Sam said, putting the magazine to one side. "I'd like to book a room, please."

"Uh-huh, okay. That's not a problem. Would you like breakfast in with that?"

"Erm, yes, please."

"Okay. If you could put your details in the book, please," he ordered, turning the guest book towards her.

Looking at it, she didn't know what to put for an address, so she put her old one in. She also used a fake name.

"Here's your key. You'll be staying in room five."

"That's lovely." Taking the key, Sam went to get her money out. "How much?"

"Oh, you pay on leaving."

"Right, I see. I'm stepping out tonight, and I might not be back until late. Will that be a problem?"

"Not at all," he said, smiling and clapping his hands together. "You have a fob on that key, which opens the main door."

"Great," she said, gathering her things, along with the magazine.

"Dinner is served at midday, with tea at six. Breakfast starts from seven tomorrow, and runs until nine. If you have any questions, please don't hesitate to pop down and give me a shout."

"Thanks," she said, heading up the stairs to her room.

When she got to her room, she hurried inside and locked the door. She then went to the curtains and drew them. Looking around her, she noticed there was a double bed in the room, which looked so comfy. Maybe I can grab an hour later? she thought.

She went into the bathroom – it was fitted with a luxurious bath complete with jets. "Oh, that looks so nice!" she whispered. Tearing her gaze from the bath, she turned around and came face-to-face with her reflection.

Her face looked death-white and thin. Her eyes looked sunken and blacked out. Her lips parted and formed an O shape. She put one hand to her emaciated cheek and started crying. Even though she had given her hair a good wash at Hob's, it still looked a mess.

Sam then removed her T-shirt and gasped. She hadn't realised it earlier, but now that she was in a safe haven, she could reflect. Her body was skeleton-thin – her boobs were non-existent. This had been the result of years of poor eating, which had all been Crystal's doing.

How could she have done it to me? she thought. I'd been so, so young. Wiping tears from her eyes, Sam continued to look at herself. She needed to drive the message home – her sister had to pay. Had to. Not only that, once tonight was over, she would have a chance to start fresh. A chance to become a new woman.

"Come on, pull yourself together!" she said, shaking her head. "What if I skip town?!" she blurted. Looking up, she stared at herself. "I mean, why not? I have money. If I left right now, I could be in a different part of the country by tonight. I could just disappear."

The thought made her sad. "No, I couldn't do that. Not with Crystal still out there. I need to put her down! It's either her or me, and it needs to be her, the fucking crazy bitch! Maybe I can look at trying to prove my innocence after tonight? Then I would be able to make a fresh go of things."

Smiling, she shook her head. "Let's just wait and see what happens…"

She turned from the mirror and a fresh thought entered her mind. Why not go down to one of the shops and get a few things? Make-up, hair colouring…That's enough to put a smile on a girl's face.

Leaving the bathroom, Sam once again entered the main room and grabbed her bag off the bed. She hung the rest of the clothes in the wardrobe before taking the money out – whoever's behind this hasn't given me that much money, she thought. "It'll do," she told herself, picking up the key to the room and heading out the door.

Standing outside the B&B, Sam spotted a chemist on the opposite side of the street. She went over to it and picked up a few things she needed, along with a few extra treats for herself. Finished in the shop, she then went next door to a newsagent's and picked up a few cans of beer, some food and a daily newspaper before heading back to her room.

When she was hidden away once again, Sam relaxed. She headed into the bathroom and started to fill the bath with piping hot water. Leaving the water to run, she returned to the main room and switched the TV on, and then she sought out a music channel. Finding Planet Rock, she then rifled through the things she'd bought whilst listening to the loud music.

After placing all the make-up and the hair dye in the bathroom, she opened a sausage roll she'd bought and popped a can open. It feels good to be eating junk and drinking crap that isn't good for you at this time of day, she thought.

Sam couldn't remember the last time beer had passed her lips – the lager was ice-cold and tasted amazing. Combined with the junk food, she felt as though she was in heaven. Once finished, she picked up the pastry she'd bought and ate that, too. Her stomach rumbled as she chewed and drank the beer in a greedy fashion.

As she was about to pop another can and eat more, she realised the bath was still running. Going to the bathroom, she switched the hot tap off, then returned to the main room. Throwing the spent can and food wrappers into the small plastic bin in the room, she opened a second lager. It tasted better than the first. With this, she opened a packet of sandwiches and a bag of crisps.

"It won't take me long to get my shape back!" she said with a packed mouth. Burping, she put the can down and concentrated on her food. When she finished, she took her can into the bathroom with her and started to fill the tub with cold water.

After a few moments of letting the cold tap run, she placed her can at the side of the bath and then stripped off. She could barely look at her body – her arms and legs reminded her of spindles, and the thicket that had grown around her pussy made her look away in disgust.

"Well, that's one thing I can cure right away!" she said, looking up at the packet of razors she'd bought from the pharmacy. "But first, let's have a nice soak." Slipping into the water, she moaned as the heat engulfed her. "That's what I'm talking about," she said between gritted teeth.

After spending close to an hour-and-a-half in the bath, Sam finally got out and shaved all the hair off her crotch. When she'd finished doing that, she cleaned the bath and dyed her hair red – a colour she had always wanted to go.

Now, standing in front of the mirror naked, with her hair done, she looked at herself. "Wow, baby, you look much better already! All I need to do now is put a bit of meat on my bones."

With a towel wrapped around her body, she proceeded to pick up her empty can and slope off into the main room. Binning the tin, she opened another and grabbed the paper she'd bought. I wonder if there's anything in here about my escape, she thought as she walked over to the bed and flopped onto it.

All she found on the front page was political news – there was nothing about the hospital. Strange, she thought. You'd think an escaped mental patient would make headline news! Maybe it was a put up job?

Someone was paid to look the other way and not cause a stink…

This could be much bigger than I first thought! Maybe others are involved, and not just me and Crystal. The more she thought about it, the more nervous she became. Thoughts of taking the money and running came back to her. Had her feelings for revenge against Crystal not been so strong, she probably would have packed up and left.

"It is what it is, I guess," she said.

Closing the paper, she noticed she'd picked up a local rag, one that only covered the town of Porthcawl. Ah, that's probably why there's nothing on my escape, she thought. Pushing the thoughts to the back of her mind, Sam continued to thumb through the paper – nothing but war, death, famine, Z-list celebrities and lying politicians. Then, something in the entertainment section caught her eye:

Porthcawl Pebble   Page 9
The Girl's Got Wood!

By Stacey Mewse

Yesterday evening at a delightful little club in the sunny town of Porthcawl, I was treated to an act the likes of which I have never seen before!

The club itself is a small one in the centre of the town and hosts a variety of different acts ranging from the seductive to the obscene to the plain bizarre. Last night's spectacle was an even measure of all three.

When I seated myself down in the dingy club interior, nestled in the protective cloak of the darkness beyond the stage, I was not quite sure what to expect. I had heard stories about the infamous act I was about to experience, but nothing could quite have prepared me for seeing it in the flesh.

The curtains opened and the lights suddenly flickered on, the crowd falling into an expectant silence around me. A gorgeous blonde strutted onto the stage, all heaving bosom and Amazonian promise. In her arms she tenderly carried a small male dummy. Her outfit brought gasps of appreciation from the men in the crowd. I knew this was Crystal. Had I not been pre-warned I would not have known what to expect…

The whole crowd watched with hungry eyes as the busty blonde launched into her first routine, a real crowd pleaser. She placed her dummy down onto a podium in the centre of the stage and folded her arms next to him, propping herself up with her back arched and her breasts pushed up. Her voice was seductive as she happily giggled and said, 'How ya doin' Harry?'

The dummy had jeered, 'All the better for being eye level with those babies, slut!' And its head had turned to motorboat those inviting mounds. I felt simultaneously jealous of it and curious as to whether she'd need help picking out some splinters later.

She pushed the dummy away and stepped back, producing a handful of phallic stress balls and proceeding to juggle them ever more skillfully whilst Harry heckled her about how she handled cocks. The crowd groaned and rolled their eyes as she quipped back that he was all talk for a man who was all wood and no action. I could have sworn I saw the dummy move as it shouted its angry reply, but it must have been the lighting. She flinched when it shouted, truly looked frightened of the consequences of her actions. That only made the whole act all the more convincing. Christ knows what she expected it to do – give her a splinter?

The raunchy show cycled through a few more titillating acts. Harry the dummy sang some filthy little ditties while Crystal seductively enjoyed a lollipop, then two, then three…all without once losing the tune. You had to commend her oral talents. Then they moved on to tell a few dirty jokes, Crystal blushing and feigning shock at every punch line.

The act flowed as though Harry was a flesh and blood human being, and the whole crowd was laughing and leering in equal measure.

The final part of the act was a quick-change routine, where Crystal used a circular pop-up curtain to hide behind whilst she changed. She cycled herself and the dummy through a range of outfits. First a suit and a cocktail dress, followed by a variety of other sexy get-ups. Eventually they finished on a tarts and vicars ensemble. From there they performed a short skit where Crystal begged to be absolved for her sins and Harry had her confess to every tiny gory detail of them, one wooden hand rubbing at his dummy's crotch. The crowd were in stitches, and there were calls for an encore. But Harry's voice insisted that he had 'other jobs' for his busty assistant backstage, and they bowed away to a chorus of good natured booing as the disappointed crowd hoped to jeer them back on stage. The dummy cackled at that, and for a moment it sent a chill down my spine…until I noticed Crystal's shapely rear sashaying off-stage.

I would recommend this show to any adult with a funny bone, though it's definitely not for the prudish. Who'd want to waste a woman like that on them anyhow?! Get yourselves down to the theatre before the show goes out of town. You won't regret it!

The energetic review enraged her – it caused Sam to spring from the bed and shred the paper into little more than confetti. "Fucking bitch!" she yelled, then swiped the lamp off the desk in front of her before throwing her make-up products across the room.

Panting, she tore the sheets off the bed and threw them about the place. Had she the strength, she would have upended the bed and thrown the TV set through the window.

Collapsing onto the bare bed, Sam rolled herself up into a ball and sobbed. "That bitch has managed to continue with her life as normal. I fucking hate you! *Hate*!" she screamed, pounding the mattress with her fist until it hurt.

When her tears were exhausted, Sam rolled onto her back and looked up at the ceiling. She dried her eyes the best she could with the back of her hand and swore revenge on her sister as she did so.

Closing her eyes, pleasant thoughts of cutting her sister's heart out filled her mind, along with thoughts of throwing Harry onto a roaring bonfire. The visions of them squirming helped her fall into a deep, dark – but beautiful – sleep…

THE SECOND ARRIVAL…

Norm had driven most of the way to Porthcawl from Hob's Cafe last night, but he had stopped off on a lay-by for a few hours of sleep. Norm, who knew the area well, had taken all the back roads to the seaside town.

With B-roads came plenty of farmland, wooded areas and quiet places to park. It was in one of these secluded little areas he'd parked for a nap. On getting into his pickup, Norm had made sure to tune in to the local radio station, but nothing of his escape seemed to have hit the news at that time. Knowing he was safe, Norm had kept the music playing as he'd drifted in and out of sleep until the sun had risen.

Now, back on the road, he was only a few miles away from his destination. When he got there, he had no idea what he was supposed to do. The letter said the party doesn't start until eight, Norm thought. I could book a room? I'm sure there was money in that envelope.

He let that thought play over in his mind as he drove. After all, I'll need to freshen up before tonight – I can't very well look like a tramp in front of my darling

Angharad. And, sooner or later, I'm going to have to dump this truck. Anyone could have spotted me by now and taken the licence plate number.

The more he thought about it, the more staying at a hotel or guesthouse made sense. What if I try to find the venue first? At least then I won't have a struggle this evening, he mused. Yes, good idea, he told himself.

Pulling off the road and into another lay-by, Norm popped the latch to the glove box and prayed his Sat-Nav was still in there. Where had the jeep been? he suddenly thought. I would have thought everything would have been taken away, once I'd been sentenced to thirty years in that hospital.

Well, Angharad is a crafty soul. God knows what she's been up to since I've been gone. As he rummaged around inside the tiny space, bits of paper, wrappers and stale cups tumbled out of it and onto the floor. "Shit," he muttered as he continued to burrow and grope.

About to give up, Norm's hand fell on the electronic device. "Yes!" he exclaimed, switching the thing on. Finding it to be dead, which was no great shock to him, he plugged it into the cigarette lighter, and the Sat-Nav's empty battery immediately started charging.

After waiting a few minutes, he again tried to switch it on. This time, the machine powered up and greeted him with a "Hello." That always made him smile. He set the electronic voice to Irish – he found it to be sexy and inviting. Not that he told Angharad that.

Not being able to find a postcode on the letter from Wadsworth, Norm put the street name in, and the Sat-Nav found it –he was precisely ten-point-four miles away. The thing gave him instructions to drive straight on before taking the fourth exit at the next roundabout.

Happy, Norm attached the small machine to his windshield so he could see and not just hear the directions. As he approached the roundabout, Norm took the fourth exit as instructed. He then turned the music to mute so he could hear what he was being told.

He liked nothing more than driving the old back roads, as the traffic was so light. The roads were that deserted, it was like having the road all to himself – Norm couldn't remember the last time he'd passed another car. He'd certainly not passed any last night as he'd made his way from the hospital to the pull-in he'd slept at.

Turning the radio up slightly, as he'd come to realise he could just watch the directions, Norm felt an icy chill soak into his bones as a flash news report came on. The reporter cut through the song that was currently playing…

"…*We interrupt the current show, as more updates have become available to us regarding the escapees from Castell Hirwaun, a hospital for the criminally insane. It was reported earlier this morning that three patients had broken out of their cells when a supposed power outage occurred within the hospital late last night…Though details are sketchy, an insider at the hospital has come forward and stated that the escapees may have had inside help…This is to be confirmed. Also, it appears that more than three may have escaped in the melee, but no names have been mentioned as of yet…The police hope to release names and images of all escaped patients later today…*"

Norm let a titter escape him. "Oh, Angharad, you are a naughty girl!" he said, keeping his eyes glued to the road. "By the time the police gather all the information, I'll be reunited with you, my beloved. Nothing will stop us – we'll skip town and head for the border," he told himself.

He had it all worked out in his mind.

Nothing would get in his or his wife's way – uh-huh. And if they did, he would cut them down with his axe. He always kept a spare one hidden under some tarpaulin in the back of the truck.

His smile widened at the thought of dismembering people.

It was fun! he remembered. The crunch of bone. The sound of blood sprinkling.

With those happy thoughts in mind, Norm started to whistle along to the song currently playing. Soon the funfair of Porthcawl came into view, but it looked quiet. None of the rides appeared to be moving. Then he remembered it was early morning – nothing would be going at this hour, he thought, and then *tutted* to himself.

The electronic guide took him past the fair and onto a busy section of road, which appeared to take him out of Porthcawl. With five miles still to travel, Norm started to think he'd put the wrong address in to his Sat-Nav. "Where the bloody hell…?" Norm started when he noticed he was being led down a country lane.

With a quizzical look on his face, he kept going. He was down to one mile of travelling left. When a lay-by came into view, Norm was about to use it to turn around, but then he saw a signpost that filled him with all the confidence he needed:

Eagle Moss Avenue/Mansion ¼ ➡

Smiling, he continued down the path until he came to the right turn. The junction took him down another path, which opened onto a residential street. On passing another signpost, he noticed it was called *Eagle Moss Av.* Looking at house numbers, he realised he was at the bottom end of the street.

Driving on, Norm stopped every now and then to

check the house numbers, which were now in the three hundreds. "Where the hell is three-seven-nine?" he mouthed to himself, noticing the houses came to an end after three-seven-eight.

Following the road around and up, he saw a signpost for *Eagle Moss Mansion,* and so he kept going. Eventually, the steep, windy road brought him to a wrought iron gate. In the distance, beyond the barred entry, lay a massive mansion. On one of the concrete pillars the gate was attached to, Norm saw the number of this house: 379.

"Okay, so now I know where to come tonight," he said, looking at the long drive, which had neatly trimmed hedges, trees and foliage either side of it. It led all the way up to the impressive house at the end, but Norm couldn't see much of it from here. "Whoever owns it must be a right flash bastard."

Norm turned his vehicle around and headed back the way he had come. "Now, if only I can find a place to check in to…"

As he made his way back onto the main road, Norm kept his eyes peeled for a place to lay low for the day. Anything would do, he thought as he drove around the area.

Spotting a pub, The Seagull Inn, which had its own car park, Norm pulled in. He couldn't believe his luck, as he was only a stone's throw away from Eagle Moss Mansion. Taking up a parking space, he turned the engine off and grabbed his bag. Inside, he found the spare cash he'd been given. "There should be plenty to get me a room for the night," he said, looking at the shabby building before him.

Getting out of his pickup, Norm went to the back compartment. He wanted to make sure his axe was still there. Seeing the tarp, he threw it back and found what he was hoping to find. His wood cutting instrument lay on its side with pride – the axe head gleamed as the sun reached it. The wooden shaft looked brand new.

Sighing, he replaced the tarp and walked over to the entrance of the pub. I could be taking a risk, he thought. What if images of me have gone public by now? They could easily capture me and turn me in!

Looking back at his pickup, he wondered if he could just sleep in it instead? But I'd need to freshen up ahead of tonight. Come on, he told himself, let's bloody well risk it. That radio report was only broadcast an hour ago – the police don't work that fast.

Entering the stale pub, a waft of beer and smoke hit him like a heavy weight punch. It caught at the back of his throat, causing him to cough. "Jesus, what a stench!" Somewhere in the distance, a Hoover worked the carpets. "I hope it's much cleaner upstairs!"

When he walked along the carpet to the reception/bar area, his feet made a crunching noise. It turned his guts, but he pushed the sounds and thoughts from his mind.

"Help ya?!" the barman asked, wiping pint glasses with a tea towel. He eyed Norm with suspicion.

Do I really look that dodgy? he wondered. Maybe I look nervous? He tried to loosen up as he smiled and walked over to the barman. "I was wondering if you had any spare rooms?"

"Yeah," the man spat. "How many nights?"

"Er, just the one. Please."

"That'll be fifty quid, mate."

"That's fine," Norm said as he counted the cash out.

"Breakfast will cost you more, mind you."

"No, I'm not looking to have breakfast."

"Fifty it is 'en!" the barman said, setting the glass and rag down. With one free hand, he snatched the money off the counter and threw a key towards Norm. "Room six. Top of the stairs." He grunted, then turned and went back to cleaning glasses.

What an ignorant bastard, Norm thought as he took the key off the counter. As he was about to turn to leave for his room, he noticed the TV was on – it was situated above the barman, who could easily lift his head and see what was on.

A breath caught in Norm's throat as it flashed up on the screen about the escape. Thank God the sound's down, he thought, watching.

"Anything else?" the barman asked.

"No!" Norm blurted, and ripped his gaze away from the TV.

As the barman turned to see what Norm was looking at, the news programme switched to something else. Norm let his clutched breath free.

"Good," the barman said, turning back to face Norm.

But Norm had already gone, and was now making his way upstairs to his room.

THE THIRD ARRIVAL...

The first thing I need to do is get rid of this fucking car, he thought. This limo is going to look a bit conspicuous when I get to a more populated area. Klaws hadn't pulled over for a rest – he'd kept going through the night, intending to get to his destination as soon as possible.

Even though he'd destroyed all the notes he'd been given, the address he was supposed to go to tonight was lodged in his head. My memory might be shit with all other kinds of information, but not addresses, he thought. I wouldn't be much of a Santa if I couldn't remember where all the naughty little boys and girls lived, now would I?

That brought a smile to his face as he sat and looked out the windshield. He'd found a disused car park, which was situated opposite Porthcawl's fairground. The car may have been big, but he'd made sure to park it between two massive bottle banks – trees and shrubbery were at the back of the car, so only the front could be seen. Not that there were many people around at the moment…

Klaws had watched the sun rise over the sea, thinking it a magical site for a Christmas morning. The ball of fire, now high in the sky, had brought with it a blue, serene sky. Gulls flew low as others picked at food on the floor and in the bins. The promenade was deserted, with the odd car passing now and then.

Klaws felt calm as he sat and watched.

What am I going to do? I have hours to kill before tonight! Well, I do have a limo. I could stretch out in the back and demolish the booze cabinet. It's well stocked, he thought, then smiled. There's even enough room for me to be able to change out of these clothes.

Hmm, that's a thought – what have I got in that bag that was given to me? Making sure to take the keys with him, he got out of the limo and sat in the back seat. Once inside, he locked the doors.

"Now, let's have a look and see what we have," he said as he tipped the bag upside down. Some of the contents spilled onto the plush leather seats whilst other bits hit the floor. With the stuff on the seat, he sifted through it – all that appeared to be there was his black Santa suit.

On the floor lay a bundle of money.

"Huh, a fat lot of good money will do Klaws," he said.

He unrolled the suit and saw there was a selection of T-shirts wrapped in it. He checked the tags – they were in his size: 4XL. "Perfect." As he thumbed through them, he noticed they all had quirky things written on them.

The first one he saw had: "I Shaved My Balls For This?!" Whilst this made him laugh, it didn't quite feel right, and so he placed it to one side. Not to say he would never wear it; it just wouldn't be right for today or tonight.

T-shirt number two was inscribed with: "Hitler was right – Doughnuts Are Delicious!" The third, which was a frontrunner, had "I'd Rather Be Snorting Cocaine Off A Hooker's Arse" on it.

"Ha-ha, I do believe I'll be wearing that one tonight," he said aloud, slapping his knee. Putting the black T-shirt with white lettering to one side, Klaws pulled a bottle of whiskey from the rack in front of him. He uncapped it and took a massive swallow.

"Ah, tastes damn fucking fine that!" he yelled, and then thumped the limo roof with his free hand.

Putting the bottle down, he looked at the last T-shirt in the pile. "Looks like the best was saved for last," he said as he set the item of clothing to one side. "Think I'll use this one tonight, instead of option number three. I'll wear that one today."

With his attire picked out, Klaws pulled his hospital top off. Hidden beneath the garment was a huge tattoo – the inked image was of an unkindness of zombie ravens, six of them in total. Flesh hung from their bloodied beaks whilst guts and eyeballs were clutched in their talons. Their eyes were crimson-orange orbs of fire; their bodies were ravaged and pulpy. Clumps of feathering had been torn from the birds.

Some were looking skyward with their beaks open in mid-screech, whilst others looked forward. Looking down at the image, Klaws had forgotten he had it or when he'd had it done.

Shrugging, he put the "I'd Rather Be Snorting Cocaine Off A Hooker's Arse" T-shirt on before slipping his hospital trousers off. I could stay in them, he thought, but I'd rather be comfy. He pulled on his black Santa trousers, but left the jacket and hat off for now.

Looking on the floor, he noticed boots had also been supplied. "Brilliant!" he exclaimed, then kicked off the slipper-sandals the hospital had issued him. With his boots on, he felt much, much better. "Time to meet my public, I think."

Getting back out of the car, Klaws stretched his back. When his bones cracked, he let out sounds of satisfaction, and then rolled his head and cracked his knuckles. Feeling loose, he stepped away from the car and pushed the little button on the fob. All the lights around the limo flashed, indicating it was locked. The car alarm set.

Pleased, Klaws made his way across the road. For some strange reason, the fairground seemed to be calling his name. *I have plenty of time to kill, and a stroll isn't going to harm me. Maybe I'll be able to find some grub along the way?* he thought, his belly rumbling.

Exiting the open-air car park, Klaws crossed the road and walked up to the gates of the fair. They were locked. "Damn it!" he said, then stamped his foot. The gate was too high to climb, and so he walked along the wall, searching for a more suitable climbing spot.

Making sure nobody was watching him, Klaws made his way around the back of the huge fairground. The wall was nowhere near low enough to scale. Even if it had been, it was trimmed with razor sharp barb, broken glass and six-inch nails.

"Don't fancy ripping my sack open on them!" he said, which was followed by a "Ho-ho-ho! You can't beat crappy Christmas jokes!"

Continuing his walk around the perimeter, Klaws came across a second gate, which appeared to be open. Beyond the gate was a ride operator, who seemed to be guarding the entrance.

From where he stood, Klaws monitored the shabby-looking man's movements. He doesn't appear to be doing much guarding! Klaws thought as he watched the man tinker with the motor of a shitty rollercoaster ride called "The Punisher."

"Charlie," the man called. "*Charlie*! Get that fucking jack out here, ya lazy fuck!"

"Coming, Dad!"

Klaws couldn't help but smile. "That's the way to keep the little fuckers in line!" he uttered.

When Charlie appeared with a jack in tow, Klaws immediately thought the boy could do with several decent meals to put some meat on his bone. "Looks as though someone has draped some clothes over a bamboo shoot!"

Sniggering, Klaws watched as father and son jacked up one section of the ride. Once enough space had been made, the father got on his back and slid under the massive machine.

"Stay there and watch that jack!" the father bellowed.

"Okay, Stan!" the son said.

"For fuck's sake, would it harm you to call me 'Dad' once in a fucking Goddamn while?!"

"Maybe. That's why I don't want to find out!"

"Fucking smart arse – you're no better than your grease-monkey father here!"

"Don't I know it!" Charlie muttered.

"What the fuck did you say?"

"Nothing."

"Good, now keep your Snicker chute shut and hand me that spanner by your feet."

When Charlie turned his back to get the spanner, Klaws made a stealth-like move through the gate and into the fairground. Nobody appears to be around, apart from these bozos, Klaws thought.

"Here you go," Charlie said, handing the spanner to his dad.

"Thanks."

"No problem."

"Oh, and do me a favour, close that gate. I meant to do it, but I bloody forgot to."

"You popped out?" Charlie asked.

"Yeah, I had to go and get a part from the car."

"Okay…"

Before the youngster could turn around, Klaws had picked up a hammer from off the floor nearby. He smashed the ballpoint part through the lad's skull. His body crumpled like a house of cards and made a sickening thud as it hit the dirt.

"Charlie, what the fuck are you doing?! You better not be fucking around…" Before he could finish his sentence, he started screaming like a girl as Klaws pushed the body of his son under the ride with him. "Charlie!"

"Ho-ho-ho!" Klaws bellowed as he released the jack.

The speed at which the machine dropped gave Stan little time to react; his and his son's heads were squashed like a couple of grapes. Squirts of blood fired from beneath "The Punisher" as Stan's legs thrashed for a few moments. His heels clicked against the gravel, which reminded Klaws of an energetic tap dancer doing his thing.

"Merry Christmas!" he spat before moving on.

What shadows there were, Klaws stayed in them, as other fairground workers rushed to see what all the noise was about. It didn't take long for all the gasps and sobs to follow.

Sniggering, Klaws moved away from his mess as quickly as he could. The last thing he heard before moving out of earshot was, "Looks to be a tragic accident, people," which made him smile all the more.

As he passed stalls and attractions aimlessly, Klaws couldn't understand what he was doing. His mind was a jumble. Where am I heading? What am I doing in here? How am I going to get out? As the questions assaulted his mind, he kept moving, not totally aware of his surroundings.

When the big top came into view, he stopped and looked up at it. His lips formed a perfect O shape as he gazed on in wide wonder. "She's beautiful!" he gasped. I need to see the inside, he thought.

Walking up to the canvas big top, Klaws tried to lift a section of it but noticed it was all pegged to the ground. "Damn it!" he said, then moved around the tent until he came to a small opening – nobody appeared to be in sight, and so he slipped inside.

"Wow!" escaped him, as he looked at all the rows of empty seats – the vastness inside was breathtaking. Looking up, he couldn't believe how high up the point of the big top was. Whilst looking, he noticed the tight ropes.

Creeping forward, Klaws had a good look around, convinced there was nobody about to catch him. As he walked to the opposite end, he used the canvas exit and found himself among rides and stalls once again.

As he was about to go back the other way, a sound caught his attention. It was coming from his left. "Hmm," he said, then moved in that direction. Rounding a corner, he noticed a few smaller tents, along with a couple of caravans and a stable for horses.

"Mr. Tickles and associates" was written across one of the tents. "Mr. Tickles?" he mouthed.

Moving closer to that tent whilst making sure nobody spotted him, Klaws pulled aside a section of canvas entryway and poked his head in. He heard a voice in the distance, and so Klaws walked in. Visibility inside was poor, as it was gloomy.

A rank odour clung to the air – it reminded Klaws of dead animals and rotting flesh. It didn't bother him in the least; rather, it further intrigued him, so he pushed on. When figures became visible, he ducked behind a few crates and peeked out.

He tried to make out the large shape standing before him, but the lighting was too poor – he needed to get closer. Creeping through the shadows, Klaws moved as close as he could. Boxes and other objects blocked his path as he went, but he managed to sidestep around them with ease, making little to no noise.

"And you trust her?" Klaws heard a voice say.

"Of course!" a second voice said. It belonged to a man, whereas the first had been a woman's. Neither of them sounded like pleasant customers, Klaws thought as he moved closer still.

When both people came into plain view, he could see it was a pair of clowns holding a conversation, and it was indeed a man and a woman. The man was huge – mountain huge – and dwarfed the fragile-looking female. Looking at them, Klaws just knew they were dangerous.

The woman looked feral, even though smudged make-up hid her face. Her eyes looked tired and wild – her hair, much like her clothes, was unkempt. He couldn't tell what the male clown looked like, as he had his back to him.

"Are you sure, Tickles?" she asked the man, who was right up close to her. He towered over her – hid her in his shadow.

"Yes, damn it!"

"Sorry!" The woman whimpered, cowering away slightly.

"You dare question your master?!" he shouted, raising his hand but not striking.

What a fucking strange pair! Klaws thought, watching them from the shadows.

"No, master. Please!"

The man-clown lowered his hand. "Good, because you know what happens when you question my authority!" he barked at her.

"Yes!" she said, getting to her knees. When she got down on the ground, Klaws noticed the woman had a collar around her throat, and the man was holding a lead.

"Have you checked on Nightshade this morning?"

She shook her head. Klaws heard the rattle of chain.

"Don't you think you should?" he demanded, unwrapping the chain from around his hand to allow the woman room for manoeuvring.

Klaws watched as the woman crawled across the hay-scattered floor – she headed off into the shadows, which were well beyond her master. Her destination appeared to be a large cage. When she reached it, she grabbed the bars and pulled herself to her feet.

"Nightshade!" she called, her tone seductive. "Wakey-wakey!"

What in the hell do they keep in that cage? Klaws thought as he watched on in amazement. I've stumbled upon a right naughty pair here…

When no answer or movement came from within the cage, the female clown picked up a tin cup and ran it back and forth along the bars, creating the most horrendous noise.

"Necrotic!" Tickles yelled. "Stop that incessant noise, woman!" He then pulled on the chain hard, causing Necrotic to choke, and then sniggered.

She raked the bars a few more times just to piss him off the little bit more.

The chain was pulled taut once again; more choking sounds ensued.

"Enough!" he barked.

"Okay, okay, master!" she said.

When a sound came from within the cage, Klaws moved closer, but still kept himself hidden behind boxes in the shadows.

A dark, standing figure moved to the bars and looked down on Necrotic. "Yes?!" came the voice. It sounded husky from where Klaws hid.

"Time for breakfast," Tickles bellowed.

"Is it night time?" the new voice asked.

"No, Nightshade, it's early morning."

"Then why wake me?" Nightshade asked.

Necrotic giggled. "You're funny!"

"You never left the tent last night. You must be starving!" Tickles said.

"Hmm, the last time I checked, I was able to take care of myself, Tickles."

"Oh, is that so?!" he asked, turning to face the cage. As he did, Klaws tried to get a better look of the man, who was starting to remind him of someone he once knew…but it couldn't be, could it?

The woman in the cage also seemed fearful of the giant clown, as she backed away from the bars slightly. "Yes, I can! I lived on the streets for decades before you found me! But I am most grateful that you took me in. That you care and worry about me as you do."

"Good. Here, eat this," he ordered, then opened her cage door and placed a steel bucket inside. The handle made a clanging noise as it struck the side of the bucket.

I'm sure I've read about this pair! Klaws said. Years ago, when I was in the asylum. There was a book…What was it called? His memory was nothing more than a foggy colander, and netting memories was a very hard thing to do, so he had never really tried until now.

Think, damn it. *Think*! He scolded himself. I'm sure I know them. Him, definitely. If only he would turn around, Klaws thought.

Whatever was in the bucket, it made soft squishing sounds as Nightshade put her hands into it. As she lifted her hands to her face, tearing and slurping sounds ensued, which stood only to heighten Klaws' growing curiosity. "What the fuck?"

"Can I have some?" Necrotic asked as she pawed at the bars like a kitty cat. Klaws expected the woman to start meowing, but she didn't, much to his disappointment.

"Of course!" Nightshade said, bending down to Necrotic. She slipped her hand out of the bucket and filled the other woman's mouth – even though the light was poor, Klaws could see that the woman's hands were drenched in blood. Chunks of God knows what clung to her flesh and fingers, but not after they'd been placed in Necrotic's mouth – she seemed to suck and lick them clean.

"Jesus!" Klaws whispered. As he went to duck down further in the shadows to make his retreat, a screwdriver, which had been on top of one of the boxes he was hidden behind, hit the floor.

"Shit!" he said, then ducked out of sight.

When the clown turned around, Klaws' heart raced. "No, it can't be!" he gasped.

Mr. Tickles growled on hearing the noise behind him. He narrowed his eyes, turned and exposed his needle-like teeth. Shuffling off the ground, Necrotic got into a standing position and stood by her master's side – she held handfuls of gathered chain, which she held close to her body.

Nightshade turned from her bucket of slop and looked out her bars.

"Do you sense a presence?" he asked the woman.

"Yes, Mr. Tickles," Nightshade said.

Somewhere off to their right, Custard squawked.

"Me too," Necrotic said.

"Who's there?!" he demanded. "If I happen to find anyone trespassing, it'll be instant death!"

Nothing. Everything was silent within Mr. Tickles' home. Not convinced, he stepped forward. Necrotic followed close behind, with Nightshade now stepping out of her cage and onto the top step of her ladder down to the ground. Her heels made slight clanging sounds as she did so.

"Well? Show yourself!" Mr. Tickles said. "If you damn children have snuck in here again, I'll bloody drown you. Little fucking shits!"

With both women now at his side, Mr. Tickles moved forward again. They all stuck close together, as any unknown dangers could be lurking – they'd had trouble in the past.

"If you're not going to come out, we're going to come in!" Mr. Tickles said, causing both women to laugh.

All three of them stopped in their tracks when a large figure stepped out of the shadows. Only the bottom half of his legs could be seen – the rest of the unknown was hidden. "I wouldn't want you to do that!" came a low voice from the shadows.

A gasp escaped Necrotic.

"Who are you and what are you doing back here?!" Mr. Tickles asked. "If you don't start supplying me with answers, I'm going to let these two lovelies loose on your fucking arse!"

The shadowy figured laughed. "Do you really think that pair could stop me? Come now. If you think that, then you are crazier than I thought!"

"Who are you?" Mr. Tickles asked, his tone becoming harsh.

"If you don't know that, then I'm certainly not going to tell you. Did you honestly think you could hide from me here?" the man asked.

"Hide from you? What the fuck are you going on about?!" Mr. Tickles could feel the control on his temper being lost.

A clicking sound to his left told him Necrotic had engaged the blade on her flick knife. She was ready to take whomever this was down.

"Yes, hide. There's no need to be shy around your associates – you know I've been trying to track you down to kill you for years. I must admit, I like your new disguise. You've given up on Christmas, I take it?"

"What? What are you on about?!" Mr. Tickles asked again, more puzzled than annoyed. "I think you have the wrong man!"

"Oh, that's what I thought at first, but then I saw your earring."

Mr. Tickles put a hand to the cutlass pendant. "And?!" he snapped.

"I have one. It's exactly the same," the man in the shadows said, all matter-of-factly.

"Look, dickhead. I'm sure many people have—"

"Oh, definitely not. You see, our mother gave them to us when we were very young, brother," Klaws said, stepping out of the shadows.

"*Huh*!" Mr. Tickles gasped and took a step back. "It can't be!"

"That's what I thought, on seeing you, *bro*. I didn't think it was possible – the last time I saw you, you were flying around the place delivering presents. Why a circus?"

"I have no idea what you mean – I was told you were dead. That you died years and years ago…!"

"This man is your brother?!" Necrotic said. "You told me you didn't have family. That you were an only child…"

"Oh, he did, did he? You have no idea that this man is Father Christmas?"

"What are you talking about?!" Mr. Tickles asked. "I've always been in the circus. You should know – you helped me run away from home. Some time after I'd left, I'd heard you'd been admitted into hospital. You killed our parents!"

"I think you are the one confused, brother. I'm Klaws, the darker version of Christmas!"

"I say we kill this fucking nutcase!" Nightshade said.

"No! He's my brother. I can't go killing him…"

Klaws stepped farther out of the darkness. "Now I know why I felt so drawn to this place. You were hiding here. I should have known."

"Look, you've got it wrong. I've never been hiding from you – I ran away from home when we were teenagers. I wanted you to come with me, but you didn't want to. You were close to Mam and Dad."

Klaws growled. "I'm not sure what lies you think you're spinning, brother. But today is Christmas Day, and you're going to die!" he shouted, moving forward.

"It's fucking June!" Mr. Tickles said. "You never were all there as a child. I spent years trying to forget about you. Years!"

"Years avoiding me, you mean."

"You're fucking crazy!"

"Ho-ho-ho! I've never been clearer of mind."

"Are you behind the letter?" Mr. Tickles asked. "Is it you that's dragging me up to that mansion this evening?"

"You also had a letter?" Klaws asked, stopping dead.

"Yes…Wait a minute, it said in the letter there would be people there I'd be interested in seeing…" He saw the way in which Klaws' face took on a mystified look. He was probably thinking the same thing.

"Mine too…"

"Then we set on each other?"

"Are you calling an alliance?" Klaws asked.

Looking at the two women, Mr. Tickles thought about it. "I suppose I am."

"I'm happy to call a truce until tonight," Klaws said. "After tonight's over, and we know what's what, we go back to being enemies."

Mr. Tickles put his hand out – he didn't want to argue any further. If he did, then someone was going to die, and he'd rather it be his brother. Tonight, when Klaws least expected it, he would bushwhack him. Maybe he could enlist the help of Crystal, along with the girls.

Klaws shook the offered hand. "A truce until tonight!" he said.

"Until tonight," Mr. Tickles repeated.

This was met by a nod of a head as Klaws backed out of the tent. When he'd disappeared through the canvas opening, Mr. Tickles rushed over to it, only to find his brother had gone.

"I can't believe it, after all these years…" he mouthed, unable to form any kind of thought pattern. It was becoming clearer and clearer what those letters were about, especially knowing Crystal had a sister heading into town. "I should have made the connection then!"

Shaking his head as he looked out across the fairground, Mr. Tickles had a sinking feeling ahead of tonight – he was sure it was going to be a killer party!

LATER THAT DAY...

"Don't you think it's about time we got up, Harry?"

"You can if you want – I may just lay here and rub my cock a bit more," he said.

"Don't you think you've had that thing played with enough this morning?"

"There's always room for more!"

"Ha-ha, you tickle me. Well, I'm going to get dressed and pop down to the shop."

"Why the fuck would you want to do that?" Rolling over, Harry grabbed a cigar off the bedside cabinet. He stuck it in his mouth and lit it. "When you could stay here, and fuck me some more?"

"*Tut*! Behave, will you? I was going to get a few things ahead of tonight."

"Such as?"

"Well, if you must know, I've run out of a few make-up products. I was also going to get a paper – I want to know if anything else has been said about the escape."

"Umm, good idea." After taking several drags on his fat cigar, Harry blew a stream of smoke out of his mouth. "Don't be long!" he told her.

"I'll try not to be. But first, I'm going to take another shower – you've made quite the mess of me, Harry!"

Once she was finished in the bathroom, Crystal threw on a pair of jeans and a T-shirt. Harry had fallen back to sleep, which made it easier for her to leave. Grabbing her bag and room key off the dressing table, she made her way out to the hallway.

Seeing that the coast was clear, Crystal walked over to the bank of lifts and pushed the button found there. It called one of the lifts down from the floor above. When it arrived, she stepped inside and rode it to the bottom floor.

"Hello!" the woman behind the reception desk said to Crystal, who looked at the woman and gave her a smile.

Getting out onto the street, Crystal took in a few deep breaths before turning left and walking down the sidewalk. It took her less than fifteen minutes to get to the town, which was crowded with shoppers, screaming children, old people and teenagers.

"Ugh, I hate town on the weekends," she uttered, and then proceeded to push past people. Her destination was the newsagent's, which was situated towards the middle of the street.

People pushing prams are the worst, Crystal thought as busy mothers rushed past and around her. The ones coming from behind managed to clip her heel, whilst the ones coming towards her barged her out of the way. None of them said sorry, nor were they upset with their actions, which riled Crystal further.

"An 'excuse me' would have been nice!" Crystal yelled after one of them. But her words were completely ignored, causing her to utter, "Fucking bitch!"

Pressing on, Crystal made it to the shop without any more drama. Getting inside, she noticed the newsagent's was small and empty. A ceiling fan whirred above her, cooling the area.

"Aw, that feels so damn nice!" she said aloud. The rushing air held her to the spot, causing her to throw her head back. This allowed the icy breeze down her top, which chilled her – her flesh prickled.

"Excuse me!" a man said from behind her.

"Why, what have you done?" she asked, not turning to look at him.

"You're blocking the way, madam!" he said, raising his voice.

"Oh, and that would never do!" she said.

Huffing, he pushed past her.

"Hey, watch it, you old bastard!"

"Please! No arguing in shop," the shopkeeper called.

"Hold on to your turban, Apu!" Crystal said. "I'm the one being pushed!" The shopkeeper didn't respond to her racial slur, nor did the man respond to her awkwardness. "Bastards!" she spat, going to the paper rack. She picked up a copy of a local rag, as all the big newspapers had sold out.

After picking up a few more items, Crystal went to the counter to pay – the fella who had been rude to her in the doorway was turning to leave, and so he gave her a scowl.

"Watch the wind doesn't change, mate, or your face will stay stuck like that!" she said, giggling. He muttered something under his breath, which Crystal couldn't quite make out. "Yeah, keep walking, big man."

"Next, please!" the shopkeeper said.

Placing her things on the counter, Crystal rounded on him next. "You could have stuck up for a lady, you know? Are there any gentlemen left in the world?!"

"Please, please!" he said. "No trouble. Pay and leave!"

"Oh, I'm going, don't you worry!" Slamming her money down on the counter, she didn't bother waiting for her change before storming back out into the crowded street. She was glad to be out of there.

"Bloody sexists!" she muttered, causing a passer-by to look at her in a strange way. "Yeah, and what the hell are you looking at?" she asked the teen mother. "Shouldn't you be at home, knocking another one out?!" She glared at the girl, who walked on as quickly as possible.

Enraged, Crystal marched to the top of the street, and elbowed and shoved as she went. A few people called after her, but she ignored them. Once at the top of the street, Crystal turned left and headed back to the hotel.

Soon, the huge building came into sight. The hotel kind of reminded her of the Overlook from The Shining; it was big and domineering, looming over the seafront. "So beautiful!" she whispered. "I wish Harry and I ran something like this. That would be nice. Give up all this acting and entertaining shite."

Getting to the lobby, she called a lift. Maybe I could convince him to start a business with me? Save some cash as planned, but put it into a seaside business instead of taking the show to London? Sounds good, but I'm not sure Harry will go for it.

After the lift's doors had completely parted, she stepped inside and stood against the back wall. The doors closed and took her to the floor she'd requested. Getting to the door of her room, Crystal opened up and stepped in. The inside felt cool, and Harry was sat by the window.

"Enjoy your walk?!" he asked, not looking at her.

"Not really, no. There are some right bell-ends out there!"

"Ha-ha! I could have told you that!"

"I wish you had – I may not have bothered going!" she said, throwing the shopping bags onto the bed. "Have you been sat there the whole time, my love?"

"Yeah, I have. I've been watching the fanny go by," he openly stated.

"*Tut*! Anything decent?" she asked, knowing her asking would give him a slight thrill.

"A few decent pairs of tits have been seen, yes. Why?"

"Harry, you know how much I love a good set!"

"Oh, so you finally admit it, do you?"

"Why, I thought you already knew," she said. She watched him as he rubbed his crotch. "You naughty boy!"

"Yeah, sounds about right."

"You do know what naughty boys get?"

"A good crack on the arse, just like a dirty bitch would get!"

Crystal giggled. "That's right."

"Then what are you waiting for?" he asked.

"What do you mean, Harry?"

"Aren't you going to spank me?!"

"But—"

"Do it!"

She flinched at his sudden outburst. "Okay…" She gingerly walked over to him and picked him up. He was unblinking. An unlit cigar jutted from his mouth.

"Well, what are you waiting for – Hanukkah?"

A snort-laugh escaped her. "No, of course not, Harry." Leading him back to the bed, she sat down and crossed her legs. Placing him over her knee, she started smacking his arse.

"Is that all you've got, oldie?!" he asked. "You're fucking tickling me, not making my dick hard!"

"Oh, so you wanted it harder, do you? Think you're a big man?!" she said, before giving him a few hard welts. "How do you like that?" she asked, giving him another dozen hard cracks. Her hand flared red, but she didn't show that it was hurting her. "You're lucky I haven't got my whip!"

"You dirty fuck!" he yelled as her hand struck him time and again.

"Now, now…Keep that kind of language up, and I'll have to wash your mouth out with soap and water, young man!" She could feel his dick stiffen against her thigh. "My, are you getting excited?"

"Don't stop!" he yelled. "Treat me like the filthy fuck I am!" He groaned and grunted when her hand connected with him a few more times. "Oh, you bitch. You dirty, dirty bitch!"

"He-he!" she giggled, and gave him a few more hard cracks across his backside. "Had enough?!"

"No!"

"You won't be able to sit down if we keep this up."

"Let me worry about my seating arrangements," he said, and then jerked as her hand walloped him again, and again, and again…

Stopping, she placed Harry on the bed.

"Hey, what do you think you're doing?!" he asked.

"Now I'm going to make you pleasure me, you naughty thing!" she said before standing up to slip her jeans off. She wasn't wearing any knickers. Lying back on the bed, she opened her legs and commanded Harry to lick her out. "Do your worst, big boy!"

She threw her head back in ecstasy as she felt his rough tongue against her clit. As he worked her, Crystal put her hands on her breasts and started moulding them. When she started groaning, she clenched her teeth to stop herself from grinding them.

"*Shit*!" She gasped as an orgasm shook her. Letting her tits go, Crystal grabbed handfuls of duvet as another pulse of pleasure shot through her. Soon, her knees were shaking – her thighs quivered. "Oh, God! Stop, Harry. *Stop*!"

"Pleading won't get you anywhere!" he said, briefly poking his head up before going back down on her.

After several intense orgasms, Harry stopped, for which Crystal was grateful – she couldn't withstand any more pleasure. "You really are a wicked young man!" she said, puffing out air. Sweat poured down her face.

"Glad I could be of a service!" he said, getting off the bed and going to the chair once again.

"I'm going to need another shower after that – I can't very well go to a party stinking of sex!" she said, erupting with laughter.

"Oh, and why not?"

"I'd embarrass myself, Harry."

"Pft, I wouldn't care."

"I'm sure you'd love it. Shall I not wear any knickers, either? Maybe I should just go naked!"

"Mmm, yes!"

"Pervert."

"And your point is?"

Crystal laughed. "True. What time is it, anyway?"

"It's a little after four," he said.

"We better start getting ready, my love."

"Huh?! We have hours, don't we?"

"Roughly three hours – we have to go and pick Mr. Tickles up, and that may take a bit of time."

"Not three hours, it won't!"

"Well, I guess not. Maybe another hour of relaxing won't harm."

"Of course not."

"I'm not really in any rush to go! I'm dreading seeing Sam. You know she's going to make an attempt on our lives, don't you?"

"Yeah, but she won't get a chance, my love – I'll do the bitch before she gets a look in, don't worry."

"I know…"

"Besides, we'll have that clown with us. I'm sure he'll help out if we find ourselves in a spot."

"True. He did seem to take a liking to me, so hopefully."

"Well, there you are. Stop fretting – no harm will come to you or me. I can't speak for others, mind you…" he said, sniggering.

Crystal smiled. "Who else do you think will be there?"

"Fuck knows. I still think it's a load of horse shit!"

"I guess we'll find out."

"Are you going to put a dress on?" he asked.

"Why?"

"Because I want you to show them legs off, that's why! Something short. You know I love your fat thighs!"

"Harry, they're not *fat*."

"You know what I mean, whore."

"Do I?" she asked, smiling. "A lady could take offence, you know?"

"Fucking 'lady' my white wooden arse!"

She shook her head. "I could be a lady, if you allowed me to be, Harry. I can be rather classy when I want to be."

"Oh, I see. Am I holding you back?"

"Don't be silly, Harry. I was only teasing!"

"Better fucking had been, too, or you'll be smiling with no fucking teeth left in your head." He lifted his fist and shook it at her.

"Please, Harry. There's no need to be like that – I was only playing."

"Don't get you knickers in a bunch, woman. I'm only teasing you. What are you dressing me in tonight?"

Settling back into an easy state, she put a finger to her chin as she thought about it. "Hmm, I'm not really sure. What were you thinking?"

"I fancy going in fancy dress – I don't want a fucking tux or suit!"

"So something fun, hey?"

"That's what I just fucking said!"

"How about sailor and sailor girl?"

"Ugh, no – we were in that garb a few nights ago!"

"Cowboy and cowgirl?"

"No!"

"Tart and vicar?"

"Hmm…I think we can do better!"

"Punks?"

"Not ever again!"

"Pirates?"

Harry gave her a cold look.

"Ninjas?!" she squealed.

"Yes!" he said, smacking his thigh. "That should be great fun."

"Not only that, but I can arm you with throwing stars. And if shit turns ugly, we can use them!"

"That's a very good idea."

"Ninjas it is then. I'll conceal a few knifes, too!" she said. "Those bastards won't know what hit them if they try fucking with us, Harry."

"I know, baby girl," he said, settling back in the chair.

Noticing him lighting a cigar and getting comfy, Crystal got off the bed and grabbed the newspaper. "I wonder if we have a review in this rag today."

"More than likely."

Putting the paper flat on the bed, she started to turn the pages. She scanned each quickly before moving on to the next, until an article caught her attention:

South Wales Gazette
Monday, the 20th of July
Ellie Piersol

Aberconway House Spree Killer Brought to Justice

Simone Berti, 28, has been taken into police custody, charged in connection with the Aberconway House murder spree that occurred five years ago near Bridgend University campus where one student was kidnapped, and five others lost their lives.

The horrific murders were discovered the following morning by a neighbour who noticed smoke coming from the house while walking his dog and called police. Although the house was a total loss, fire fighters arrived in time to halt the spread to neighbouring buildings.

Upon discovering the nature of the deaths inside the house, police canvassed the area for witnesses. It was during this initial investigation that Penny Davies, a clerk at the nearby co-op, reported seeing a silver Fiesta leaving the scene, operated by a dark-haired young man, when she arrived for her early bakery shift around 4:00 a.m. That Fiesta was later reported stolen.

"I remembered him, sure. There aren't too many out and about at that time of day, and he was right handsome enough to catch anyone's eye. I saw him clear as anything when he drove under the streetlamp at the corner, there, headed north. Him and the girl he was with. I feel terrible now for thinking how lucky she was to be with such a good-looking bloke, then come to find out he was a madman. Poor, poor girl."

Autopsies of the five victims proved that they'd been killed prior to the fire being set. It wasn't until news of his description spread, however, that Berti came under suspicion for at least four other disappearances and multiple other accounts of attempted kidnapping. The girl taken that night from Aberconway house, Toni Clark, has never been found.

Police are hopeful that now that Berti is in custody, faced with life in prison, further admissions of truth may yet be forthcoming.

Inquiries into Berti's past have turned up indications of a broken home and a sealed juvenile record. His mother, an exotic dancer, hanged herself some ten years ago. There is no record of his father's whereabouts, nor of his sister's, after she was reportedly removed from the home due to some sort of abuse.

For nearly a year after the tragedy at Aberconway House, no sightings were reported. Over the past four years, however, occasional reports have surfaced that have rung alarm bells with authorities.

Investigators are still piecing the stories together, but what has emerged thus far bears a macabre resemblance to another killer, Ted Bundy, whose murderous acts spanned seven states in America in the 1970's.

Like Bundy's victims, all five of the dead in Aberconway house, according to Police Chief Doyle, appeared to have been first immobilized by blows from a blunt object, and later strangled.

The reports which have trickled in over the past four years also show ominous similarities to Bundy's spree. In several cases, Berti appears to have attempted to lure his victims into his vehicle by playing at being injured and needing help.

Most disturbing of all, sources indicate that some information provided by Berti in his initial interviews with police have led investigators to look into exhuming the bodies of two of the most recently discovered murder victims thought to be connected to his case. When asked what they hoped to discover, one source close to the investigation pointed to Bundy's acts of necrophilia. If Berti was indeed copycatting the American serial killer, additional charges may be filed.

"Well, bloody hell!" she said.
"What is it?"

Turning the paper so Harry could see the piece in the paper, she said, "I knew this guy from years back – his mother used to work with me."

"Work with you?"

"Yeah, at Bunnies."

"The strip joint?" he asked.

"That's right – he was such a sweet little boy."

"Not according to that article!" Harry said.

Gosh, you grew up to be a handsome guy, didn't you? she thought, looking at the photo of Simone in the paper. Whatever happened to you? A pang of sadness rose in her as her past came crashing back. How I loved working that club. Pushing the thoughts to the back of her mind, she pressed on with looking through the paper.

Not finding anything, she flipped it back to the first page, where another article caught her eye. Somehow, it had managed to elude her the first time. As she started reading it, her flesh turned cold:

Mysterious Murderer
Massacres Married Pair

By Elizabeth Dale

Bodies of Local Couple Found in Fire; Foul Play Indicated

Fire crews were called to Hob's Cafe and Pub near Hirwaun, South Wales early this morning by would-be breakfast goers. By the time fire-fighters arrived on scene, the building was a complete loss. Two bodies have been discovered inside, believed to be the Cafe's owners, Hob and Bella Daniels. Police say there is some evidence the couple were dead before the fire started.

Fire Chief Richard Evans stated that it appeared the fire had started more than an hour before the Cafe was scheduled to open for business. He said the only vehicle in the parking area not belonging to the customers who sounded the alarm belonged to Mr. and Mrs Daniels.

He declined to comment further until police crews were cleared to enter the premises and examine the evidence.

This is a developing story. Please continue to check the Gazette online for updates.

Update 10:00 a.m:

At approximately 9:30 a.m., the fire at Hob's was sufficiently contained and the building declared safe enough for investigators to enter.

According to Fire Chief Evans, the bodies of Mr. and Mrs Daniels were able to be positively identified, despite their burned condition, by virtue of specific medical conditions identified by their physician in Swansea.

When Chief Evans was queried about the cause of the fire, he burst out, "Bloody tragic. That poor woman's body, thrown on the stove. That's what started the fire. She was dead, though. Had to have been dead." Chief Evans refused further comment and walked away making the sign of the cross.

We spoke with Miss Megan Baker, a waitress at Hob's.

"I was just coming to work," Miss Baker said. "It was only my third day, and honestly, I was thinking about giving notice. Much as I need the job, this place gave me the willies."

When asked to elaborate, Miss Baker would only say, "It was just so strange here. And there was this one fella, well, he went back to the kitchen for some reason the other night and just a few minutes later he ran out, looking scared. Said something about *changing his mind*. I don't know what he meant, but it really scared me. Plus, I think that bloody jukebox was haunted or something. The songs never sounded spot on."

Police at the scene were unwilling to comment pending further investigation.

This is still a developing story. Please continue to check the Gazette online for updates.

Update 12:15 p.m.:

The Gazette was able to secure an interview with a source close to the fire crew on condition of anonymity, as the investigation is ongoing. Please be advised, the information that follows is graphic in nature and may be upsetting to some readers.

According to our source, the fire commenced about the body of Ms. Bella Daniels, who was placed atop the stove burners in the kitchen area. Based on the condition of her remains, officials suspect she was severely beaten before being burned. Among other apparent injuries, one arm, our source stated, was shattered at the wrist and shoulder, and her skull was fractured in several places.

Further, our source divulged that the body of Mr. Hob Daniels was found where he was killed, his head smashed into the jukebox. The pattern of the fire indicated he likely did not move from the spot, and thus was most likely killed first.

The level of violence seen in the attacks was disturbing, our source indicated. In years of service, they had seen nothing comparable.

Many residents of the area have expressed concerns over Hob's in past months. Police have been called to break up fights on several occasions, and a missing girl, University student Jessica Parsons, was last seen leaving the cafe not long ago. There is no word yet on Miss Parsons' fate.

According to the latest from police, no firearms were used in this morning's attack. Pending autopsies will provide proof of the exact time and cause of death of the two victims.

Police have named no suspects at this time but are expected to hold a press conference later this afternoon to share any information they are able to discern about the possible perpetrator or perpetrators.

Please continue to watch the Gazette online for further details as this story unfolds.

Update 4:00 p.m.

Police Chief Alistair Taylor and Fire Chief Richard Evans commenced their press conference in the lobby of

Town Hall at 3:30 this afternoon. Statements were as follows:

Chief Taylor: "At approximately 5:45 this morning, a person or persons unknown entered Hob's Cafe and Pub. Inside were owners Ms. Bella Daniels and Mr. Hob Daniels.

It appears that Mr. Daniels was in the main area of the restaurant and was the first to encounter the assailant or assailants. Apparently, Mr. Daniels was overpowered and killed first. Autopsies are still pending, but our preliminary investigation suggests he was killed by blunt force trauma to the head, the murder weapon being the jukebox on the premises.

We believe that Ms. Daniels then came upon the scene, whereupon she was also attacked. We suspect her injuries were caused by a baseball bat similar to the one she and Mr. Daniels kept to hand as defence. The bat was not found at the scene, but we do not know at this time if it was removed from the premises or destroyed by the fire.

Again, although we are awaiting confirmation from the coroner, we believe Ms. Daniels had already perished from her injuries by the time her body was placed upon the lit stovetop and the fire ignited.

At this time, we do not have any solid leads as to the person or persons who committed this heinous attack. We encourage anyone in the vicinity at the time who may have seen a person or vehicle of interest to come forward as soon as possible. All information is necessary and vital, no matter how insignificant it may seem.

Until we are able to identify and detain the person or persons responsible, we encourage everyone to be watchful and practice common safety strategies. Lock your doors and windows. Notify your neighbours if you are going on holiday. If you observe strange or unusual activities, please contact local authorities at once.

We will continue to keep you appraised as this situation develops. We will take a few questions at this time."

One reporter asked:
   Q: "Does this have anything to do with reports of suspicious activities at Hob's?"

Police Chief Taylor answered, "We know of no connections between this morning's events and any previous police calls to the Cafe. Rest assured, those events will be reviewed and scrutinized closely."

Q: "Has any further progress been made on the disappearance of Miss Jessica Parsons, and do you think there is any connection?"

Chief Taylor: "To our knowledge, Miss Parsons is still missing, and again, we currently know of no connections, but will continue to investigate."

   Q: "Was any accelerant used to start the fire?"

Chief Evans: "No. The fryer was nearby and full of grease. It's probable that flames from Ms. Daniels' person reached the fryer and that acted as all the accelerant needed."

Gazette Reporter:

Q: "Chief Evans, we've received an as yet unsubstantiated report that there was an incident at Castell Hirwaun last night, that some staff may have been attacked or even killed, and that an inmate or inmates may have escaped. Is it possible Mr. and Mrs. Daniels were killed by escapees from the Asylum?"

Chief Taylor: "At this (ahem) time, we have no -- official report of an incident at Castell Hirwaun. At such time as any such information should be reported, you may be certain it will be shared promptly. Public safety is, as always, our priority.

"Let me reiterate, at this point in the investigation, we are still gathering evidence. We strongly encourage anyone who may have seen anything at all this morning to contact police as soon as possible, and as per usual to practice common sense safety measures.

"Any and all relevant information will be shared with the public promptly. Keep tabs on your local news sources for the latest updates. Rest assured your police force is, as always, vigilant and on the job. Thank you all for your time."

Please continue to check the Gazette online for updates.

Crystal lowered the paper. She knew the café only too well – it had also been mentioned in *White Walls and Straitjackets*. "Harry, something very weird and fucked up is going on!" Nothing feels real anymore, she thought.

"What now?!" he snapped. Again, she turned the paper to him. His jaw slackened, and she could tell by the look on his face that he too recognised the café and the name of the owner. "This has got to tie in to us, Sam and the letters!" he stated.

"I know, and we're going to find out what the hell is going on this evening. And if any fucker dares get in our way, then I'll kill the bastards!" she said. "Nobody, and I mean *nobody*, is getting in our way, Harry." She then balled the paper up and threw it in the bin. "I'm taking a shower," she said, slamming the bathroom door shut.

Harry continued to stare out the window. He was unmoving and unblinking. The cigar in his mouth was unlit.

Coming out of the bathroom with one towel wrapped round her head and one round her body, Crystal hummed. After grabbing her make-up, she sat down on the bed with a mirror and started to apply her "war paint", as Harry called it.

"You could have taken me in to the shower with you, cunt!"

"Harry! You know I dislike that word."

"Well? You could have!"

"Okay, I'm sorry – I didn't think! Besides, we haven't got much time to mess about. I want to be out of here for six-thirty."

"Fine, but you owe me a shower with you tonight."

"We might not be back!"

"Tomorrow, then! You aren't getting out of it, bitch."

"What I mean, Harry, is we may not be back at all – we could be dead in a ditch in a couple of hours' time!"

"Fuck off, will you – nothing like that will happen to us, mark my words."

"I'm scared shitless, and I don't mind telling you."

"We'll be fine. Between me, you and the clown, we'll ward off any threat. Your sister's nothing more than a scrawny little shit!"

"I just want to get this fucking thing over and done with, Harry."

"I'm not going to let any harm come to you!"

She stopped what she was doing and looked at Harry – it was the warmest thing he had probably ever said to her. Her heart felt as though it was ballooning in size; her mouth felt dry. She knew he loved her, but he never showed it. "Likewise," she said as she tried to swallow the lump in her throat.

Once she'd applied her make-up, Crystal stood up and fetched her hairdryer before sitting back down on the bed. Removing the lamp's plug from beside her bed, she plugged the dryer's in. It took her less than twenty minutes to get it dried and curled to a level she was pleased with.

"Fuck, I love it when you do you hair curly. You're smokin', woman!"

"Harry, you say the sweetest of things," she said. "Besides, I think it'll look nice with my dragon robe."

"Me ninja, you Japanese lady – sexy!" he declared.

"He-he, you know it." Once she'd finished with her hair, Crystal got off the bed and went to Harry. "Come on, let's get you dressed."

"*Phwoar*! I love it when you talk dirty."

She rolled her eyes as she placed him on the bed. After stripping Harry to his underpants, Crystal went over to her large trunk, which held props and clothing –

it had "Crystal and Harry's Stand-Up Show" written across the front of it in coloured lettering. Grabbing an armful of clothes she needed for Harry, she went back to the bed and started to dress him.

"I can dress myself, you know!"

"Oh, I know that – I just thought you loved me doing it?"

"You know me so well. Are you going to Talc my arse and balls, hmm?"

"Do you want me to?"

He nodded. A smirk emerged as she put her hand down his underwear. "*Ugh...*" he groaned as she eased her hand around him. "You dirty fucker!" he said.

"There you go, all nice and clean." Harry could only groan with satisfaction as she removed her hand.

After dusting her hand free of Talc, Crystal started to dress Harry in the mini, dark-coloured Shinobi shōzoku uniform – it was made from a type of keikogi cloth. She firstly put on his jika-tabi boots and socks, then slipped on the special trousers with double-ties that fastened at his ankles, knees and waist.

With his bottom half done, Crystal slipped his jacket on, which had overlapping lapels that tucked into the trousers. Once it was secured, she then put on his protective arm-and-hand sleeves – mini spikes poked out of the sides, adding a defence and attack.

"Put my hooded cowl and mask on!" he demanded.

"Give me a chance, Harry."

"Less of the backchat!"

"You want to know something – traditional ninjas didn't wear masks."

"What is this – a fucking history lesson?!"

"Sorry, I just thought you'd like to know."

He gave her a hard gaze.

Ignoring him, she put on his black hooded cowl and mask before attaching the obi belt round his waist. Hanging from the belt was a miniature grappling hook, blow pipe and Nunchaku. "There, all done!"

"Tuck some throwing stars inside my jacket. Knuckledusters, too!" he said.

Nodding, she complied with his request. "I think I'll be taking a knife with me, Harry. God knows what or who we are going to come up against tonight."

"Good idea. How do I look?"

"You look awesome – Crystal's little warrior!"

He smiled at her remark.

Putting him back in the chair, Crystal started getting herself dressed by firstly putting on clean underwear. She then slipped into the dragon dress, which was more Chinese style than Japanese, but that didn't matter.

Zipping the dress up, she turned to Harry. "What do you think?"

"Like a million!"

She smiled.

"Come on, we better get out of here – it's almost six-twenty-five."

Gathering up Harry, her purse and the room key, she headed out the door and down to the lobby. Once there, she headed through the hotel entrance, which led to the car park and their van.

They got in and Crystal headed out onto the main road. The fair was in the near distance and jumped with activity: the place was aglow as rides swooped, rose and fell.

As Crystal powered her van toward the psychedelic rendezvous to pick up Mr. Tickles, her heart sank. A pain developed in her guts. In less than two hours, she would be face-to-face with her sister, a woman who not only hated her but also wanted her dead. Gripping the steering wheel tighter and tighter, she tried to force all the negative thoughts out of her mind as she neared the fairground. But then Harry spoke, which helped take her mind off things.

"Where are you thinking of parking?"

"As close to the fair as possible."

"They have that car park opposite. Is it open at night?"

Harry seems unusually calm, she thought. He didn't seem to have his arrogant, hostile away about him. Was he, too, rattled by all this? Shit, who wouldn't be? As soon as I see Sam, I'm going to stick my knife in her. The butcher blade she had concealed beneath her dress felt weighty against her.

"I'm not really sure, Harry, to tell you the truth." As she closed in on the car park Harry had in mind, Crystal could see it was open. On a board close to the front, it had the opening times: from May through to September, the Pay'n'Display zone was open until one A.M. "Perfect!" she said as she pulled the van into a parking space.

"How long are you going to be?" he asked.

"Are you not coming with me?"

"No," he said flatly.

"Okay, suit yourself. I'll probably be about thirty minutes. Are you sure you won't come? You'd love to see Miss Sideshow Nightshade," she coaxed.

"Yeah, and why's that?"

"Didn't I tell you earlier?"

"No, you fucking didn't!"

"She's a vampire," Crystal said as she clapped her hands together.

"Aha-ha-ha-ha!" Harry burst out laughing. "You'd buy an old bullshit, fair play to you!"

Crystal looked wounded, as she lowered her gaze. "Well, if you're that sure, come and have a look for yourself. I saw her eating meat and drinking blood last night!" she said, although she wasn't one-hundred percent sure of it.

"Really?!" Harry said, showing mild interest.

"Yeah, and if you don't come along and see her now, you may not get the chance to!"

"Why, isn't she attending?!"

"I don't think so," Crystal said, again not sure of her facts.

"Hmm…Maybe I will come, then."

"You won't be disappointed, I'm telling you!"

"Come on then, let's get going," Harry said.

Crystal nodded, got out, and went around to his side of the van. Opening the door, she picked him up and cradled him in the crook of her left arm as she locked the doors with her right hand. "Right, let's hot-foot it over there…He's probably waiting for us now," she said.

As she walked through the open-air car park, something caught her eye. Turning her head to the left, Crystal noticed a limo parked between two huge recycling bins. "Strange," she said aloud.

"What is?!" Harry asked.

"There, look." She nodded with her head. "A limo."

Harry shrugged his shoulders. "And?!"

"Don't you find it odd?"

"Why? It's just a fucking car!"

"It looks like it's been parked there on purpose. As though it's been hidden out of sight…" she said, letting her sentence trail off.

"Stop reading into things – you're jumpy, that's all."

"Yeah, maybe," she said, letting the matter go.

Crystal gave the car one last look before exiting the car park and crossing the road to the fair. She didn't know why, but the sight of that limo and the way it was parked gave her the creeps.

THE GATHERING

After passing out on the bed earlier in the day, Sam had woken up in a panic – "I'm late!" she'd yelled, but then realised it had only been six o'clock.

Now, at exactly five-minutes-to-seven, she was dressed and ready to go. She jumped off the bed and cleaned the room before binning all the clothes she had used that day.

If I don't make it back to the room tonight, then I need to make sure I don't leave any evidence behind, she thought. If I die, then it wouldn't matter either way. However, Sam wasn't about to take any risks.

"If I do make it out of there tonight," she said aloud whilst looking at herself in the mirror, "then I won't be coming back here – I'll get a bus or hitchhike a lift out of town. By morning, I'll have clear daylight between me and this one-eyed place."

Looking at her watch, she noted it was gone seven. The taxi will be here any minute now, she thought as she fidgeted with her dress. Sam pulled it this way and that, as it didn't quite fit.

It's tight more than anything, she thought, looking at the way in which her boobs pushed the fabric out. At least it makes my tits look bigger than they actually are! she thought, smiling, and then pulled the dress down so it was below the knee.

She didn't like showing too much leg. Not these days, anyway. From all the prodding and testing she had gone through at the hospital, cuts and bruises had been left on her skin. Some had faded to nothing, but others remained prominent.

Not that anyone is going to be giving me filthy looks. Chance would be a fine thing, she thought, looking at her sunken face. Never mind – a few good meals and some sunshine will sort me.

Get a bus out of town! her mind screamed.

I wish I could, but I need to finish this business with my sister once and for all.

With her dress right, Sam picked up her bag, which contained the money and a concealed knife, and headed out the door. When she got outside, a taxi was pulling up to the curb. The driver's side window was down, allowing the driver to speak to her.

"Jenny?" he asked. "Jenny Miles?"

"Yes, that's me!" she answered, walking up to the taxi's passenger door. Jenny Miles was the fake name she'd used when booking her room earlier in the day. She'd always loved the name Jenny, and Miles had been taken from her favourite actress, Vera Miles.

"Cool," the driver said.

He has an Islamic look to him, Sam thought as she climbed into the back of the car. Very dishy, too. She gave him her best smile in the rear-view mirror, but he shrugged it off. What man is going to fancy a woman who looks like Skeletor's daughter? she thought, sadly.

"Where to, please?"

"379 Eagle Moss Avenue, please," she said with a scowl.

The driver appeared to smirk at her, but Sam didn't say anything. She didn't want to draw any unwanted attention just in case someone recognised her as an escapee from Castell Hirwaun.

By now, her picture could be circulating on all the news channels across the country. Her name could be being mentioned half-a-dozen times an hour on radio and TV. She was a wanted woman, so causing big scenes was definitely a big no-no on the streets.

When she got Crystal alone or with a bunch of likeminded people, she could flip out as much as she wanted. Until then, she had to keep a lid on things. She just muttered *"You blacky cunt"* under her breath.

"Excuse me?" the driver said, looking in his rear-view.

"Huh? Oh, nothing…" she said, turning her head to look out the window. Inside, she let out a massive laugh.

After a few minutes of driving, they appeared to be leaving the town behind, which alarmed Sam. Was this guy really a taxi driver? What if it's a set-up? He could be working with Crystal or even the person who sent me the letters…Her mind ran amuck as she started to breathe heavily. Sweat broke across her brow.

Keep calm, she told herself. Easy does it. Just…"Excuse me, but where are you taking me?!" Her tone was borderline hostile. It wouldn't take much to tip her over the edge. Opening her bag, she put her hand to the haft of the knife inside. She was more than prepared to punch it through the back of his seat.

"I take you to where you ask to go!" he barked. His CB radio crackled violently at that point, which sent shivers down the back of Sam's neck – she'd always hated screechy-scratchy sounds.

"Then why are you taking me out of town?!" she demanded to know. "Don't you know where you are going?" Her finger hovered over her panic button. A voice at the back of her mind screamed, "*Push it*!"

"This is the right way – you look at the Sat-Nav!" he demanded. "Do you want to bloody drive? Do you?!" he shouted.

"Oh, I…" she started to apologise after looking at the electronic map. Her face flushed. "I'm sorry…I thought…"

"Please, let me do the driving!"

"Jesus, you don't have to shout. I was just worried you were taking me the wrong way, that's all." She zipped her bag closed as violently as she could, which did little to stem her rage. "Fucking bastard!" she said under her breath.

He said nothing, just stared ahead with a hard gaze.

He's going to think I'm nuts! Let him. Once I get out of this fucking car, I'm gone. History. He'll never hear of or see me again.

When he signalled off the main road, her heart started to race once again, but then she saw a sign indicating the way to the mansion. Soon after, they turned onto a housing estate, which led to her destination.

Night has settled in fast, she thought after getting out of the car and paying the cabbie. Storm clouds had gathered above her – a rumble of distant thunder could be heard. Flickers of lightning followed shortly afterward.

"Jesus, it looks like Frankenstein's guest house!" she said just as a crack of thunder ripped the heavens open – this gave way to fat drops of rain, which started falling rapidly. She pressed the buzzer on the gate that caused it to open for her. A static voice followed.

"Please, enter!" The tone sounded joyless.

"Wadsworth?!" she said into the speaker, but nobody answered.

Stepping through the gates, she rushed up to the house. Before she rang the bell, Samantha tried to steady her racing heart as she fluffed her hair and straightened her dress. An image of Crystal filled her mind. Her legs turned to jelly. She'll fucking kill me! she panicked. She straightened and turned away from the door. I don't think I want any part of this.

Before she could make her way down the steps and back to the path, the door opened behind her.

"Why, Miss Saunders, do come in. I've been expecting you!" a lame voice croaked. She expected a burst of harsh laughter, but it never came. "Please, step inside – I'd hate to see that dress ruined."

Turning slowly, she was almost too scared to face the person who stood at her back. A scream lodged in her throat, but it would have been wasted, as a slim, plain-looking man smiled at her.

"You're normal!"

"What were you expecting, Frankenstein's monster?" he asked. She gaped at him. "Please, come in. You're the first to arrive." Stepping backwards, he pulled the door wide.

When Sam disappeared into the large house, the door closed. The next guest was awaited.

* * * *

Getting out of the shower, Norm slipped into a pair of clean pants and socks after towelling himself dry. He hated that sticky, clingy feel clothes had on the skin after showering. It caused him to sweat profusely, which led him to soak through a shirt or T-shirt rapidly.

In preparation, however, he'd opened all the windows in the room, which had worked a treat, as it allowed his body to cool-off before starting to dress. There's nothing worse than trying to put socks on damp feet, he thought.

With his pants and socks on, he stood up and got his trousers on, followed by his shirt. As he did up the bottom buttons, he suddenly realised he hadn't put any deodorant or aftershave on, and so he moved to the bathroom to do so. Once done, he finished with his shirt and moved back out to the main room.

Once there, he slipped his jacket on and pocketed his room key. Looking about, he made sure he wasn't forgetting anything. Spotting the money, he went to it and put it in the opposite pocket to his room and pickup keys.

He didn't really know what to do with the clothes he had taken off, as he probably wasn't going to see them again after tonight. Once I have Angharad back in my arms, I shall be taking her home. Then again, why not take everything with me – I have the pickup? Nah, I'll need to pop back here to checkout anyway. I'll get them then.

Happy with his choices, Norm eyed his watch and left the room. I need to get going – I hate being late.

Outside, the sky had turned dark – storm clouds were moving in. A chill stirred the night air. If the mansion wasn't such a distance, I could have walked it, Norm thought as he trotted over to his pickup.

I can't wait to see my Angharad…

Getting into his truck, Norm adjusted his rear-view mirror before putting his seatbelt on. Once he was ready, he kicked the engine to life, which started on the first turn of the key.

Smiling, he pulled out of the car park and headed out of town. With his Sat-Nav on and set to take him to the last place he had driven to, Norm got moving. But he was surprised at how little he needed the map's help, as he pretty much remembered the route.

Before making the turn for the housing estate, fat drops of rain started to pelt the windshield, forcing Norm to activate the wipers. After driving through the estate, he soon came upon the mansion. The poor lighting and rain gave the old-looking mansion an eerie effect, Norm thought as he drove up to the gate's buzzer.

"Yes?!" a voice croaked on the intercom.

"Er, it's Jenkins, Norm," he said, used to having to say and hear his name in reverse at the hospital. The outside world was lost on it.

"Ah, Mr. Jenkins – we've been expecting you!"

"Is Angharad with you?" he asked, his voice shaky with panic.

"Please drive through the gate, Mr. Jenkins. All will be revealed…"

"I'm doing no such thing! I want to know if my wife is there."

The voice on the intercom sighed. "Mr. Jenkins, what further proof do you need? I've already told you she's here – what would I have to gain from lying? Why would I break you out of a hospital for no good reason?"

"I…Er…You've got a point, I guess."

"Please, drive through the gates and park at the front of the house – we'll be at the door to greet you."

"You said 'we'?"

"Correct," the voice said, irritation evident.

"Who's *we*?!"

"Mr. Jenkins, please, just drive up to the house. I wish you no harm, only to reunite you with your wife."

The intercom cut off, leaving Norm to stare at it through the now hammering rain. "Hello?" he tried, but nobody spoke back. When the sound of clanging metal filled his ears, Norm looked out the windshield – the gates were slowly opening.

Putting his hands to the wheel, he gulped and shifted the pickup into first gear. He took it slowly, as the path before him was poorly lit. The only light available shone from the windows of the mansion.

Not even the lights on this pickup are doing that much! he thought as butterflies fluttered around inside his stomach.

Deep breaths, he told himself, as he breathed in and out, in and out...It's only Angharad and a few of her friends. But why here? Why not lead me home? His fevered mind tried to search for answers, but couldn't. I'm sure she has her reasons.

Content, Norm parked as close to the front door as possible without hitting a wall or potted plant. Happy with where and how he was parked, Norm switched the engine off. For a moment, he just sat there and looked up at the lighted windows before him. It looked inviting.

I wonder if Angharad is behind that one? he pondered. I shouldn't be just sitting here like a lemon! My beloved is awaiting me.

But he couldn't move. Not yet. He found the sound of the rain on the roof rhythmic and calming. It helped clear his head and saw off the butterflies. Counting to three, he closed his eyes and took in a deep gulp of air before releasing it and getting out of the truck.

He didn't bother locking the pickup as he made a run for the stone steps leading up to the mansion's main entrance. As he reached for the brass knocker, the door opened a crack, causing Norm to take a few steps back.

The doorway filled with a warm, glowing light, which spilled out of the house and covered Norm. He squinted slightly, but soon the bright light was obstructed, as a man filled the entrance.

"Mr. Jenkins?" the figure asked.

"Yeah…yes!"

"Would you like to follow me into the drawing room, please?"

"Wadsworth?" Norm asked, not really sure where the name came from.

"At your service," Wadsworth said, giving Norm a slight bow.

"You're not what I was expecting!" Norm said. He was scared. What was he doing here? Where were his doctors and nurses? He started to shake. "Where's Angharad?"

"She's waiting for you in the drawing room, sir. Please, step this way," Wadsworth said, opening the door fully. "Don't keep her waiting any longer."

Hesitant, Norm stepped over the threshold. The door closed at his back, which gave him a start.

"My, you look a trifle wet, Mr. Jenkins!"

"Huh? Oh, I'm okay. Honestly. My wife?"

"Firstly, can I ask – were you treated well by my loyal servant Hob?"

"Er, yes…He was very pleasant."

"Splendid. That makes two out of three happy campers!" Wadsworth said, a wide grin on his face. "Please, won't you come through and dry off, sir? Your wife and one other are waiting."

"I—" Norm was about to say with his hand up in the air to protest, but Wadsworth turned and walked away, causing him to follow in a tentative way – his footsteps were child-like as he followed after the well-dressed butler.

When Wadsworth reached a door in the massive reception area, he opened it and invited Norm over. "In here, Norm, please. This is where the guests will be gathering, so you can mingle before dinner."

Walking over to the door and peering into the grand room, he could see a scrawny woman standing by a roaring fireplace. She held a glass of sparkling white wine in her bony hand.

"That's not my wife!" Norm said. Rage built inside his guts, which knotted into a ball of fire-ice. "You said Angharad would be here!" His voice rose as he got into Wadsworth's face, but the butler didn't seem fazed.

"Please, Norm, calm yourself! She's over there," the butler said, nodding in the direction of the window.

Turning to look, Norm could see his wife in her wheelchair. She had her back to him as she watched out the window. "Angharad!" he gasped.

"I was wondering when or if you were going to turn up!"

"I wouldn't have missed this opportunity for the world…They told me you were dead. That you were all in my mind!"

"Will you stop your sniffling and get over here? You really are quite pathetic, aren't you? Just like all men – they need neutering. Looking after. I'm not sure little boys become anything more than little boys!"

Norm lowered his head as the other two looked at him in astonishment. "Sorry, Angharad," he murmured as he shuffled over to her.

"And no more womanizing, you hear me?!"

"No, of course not, Angharad. You're *all* the woman I need." Standing over her shoulder, he looked down at her. Her toothpick-like body was covered with an ugly brown-yellow colour, which saddened Norm – even the substitute limbs he'd given her had withered. No hair remained on her head, which was nothing more than skull. The bone didn't shine white, as it was mottled with an earthy radiance – her clothes were a tattered, moth-eaten mess. "Oh, my love, you have not been looking after yourself as you should," he told her.

Behind him, Samantha spoke to Wadsworth. "What the hell is wrong with him? Doesn't he know she's de—"

Wadsworth stopped her in her tracks. "Please, my dear, can't you see Norm is having a tender moment with his wife?"

Norm faced them. "Who are you?" he asked Sam.

"Er...Sam. Samantha, that is!" she said, taking a nervous sip of wine.

"All will be revealed, Norm, I can assure you – let's just wait until the others arrive," Wadsworth said.

"You do realise my sister and I are going to go at it, don't you?! I plan to kill her on sight," Sam said.

"My dear, it will not come to that – I have not gathered you so you can kill one another."

"We shall see about—"

"I can assure you, it *won't*!"

"What makes you so sure?" Sam asked.

"For a start, I will not tolerate it! Secondly, I know something about you all that you will all want to know. Secrets will be revealed!" he said, and a huge smile graced his face. "Many a surprise awaits you."

"*Norm, what the fuck is this crack-pot talking about?!*"

"I have no idea, love. What do you mean, 'secrets'?" Norm asked.

"All in good time, Norm..." Wadsworth said. "Now, would either of you like another drink? I need to check on the cook and preparations for this evening."

"No thanks," Sam said.

"I'll have a beer, if you have one?" Norm said.

"Coming right up, sir!" Wadsworth said, then left the room.

* * * *

As Crystal walked through the fair with Harry tucked under her arm, people swarmed about her like flies. The stench of sweat mixed with candyfloss, frying onions and meat was overpowering her sense of smell and crushing her nostrils.

"Fuck sake, haven't people got anything better to do than hang around a child's amusement park of an evening?!" she uttered as people shoulder-barged, elbowed and shoved past her with excitement.

Crystal wasn't interested in the rides, prizes, bright lights or food – all she wanted to do was get to Mr. Tickles so she could get him into the van and moving. The party would be starting in just under an hour, and she hated being last in line.

"Do you have to fucking rush?!" Harry asked. "I'm getting hit left, right and fucking centre here, woman!"

"Please, Harry, we're almost there. I hate this shit as much as you do!"

"Didn't you know talking to yourself is the first sign of madness, love?!" someone called from the crowd. A few *whoops* went up around them.

"Very funny, dickhead," she muttered under her breath.

Harry giggled.

As she continued to storm through the fairground, the big top came into sight, which gave here a feeling of relief. Not only were the crowds getting thicker the deeper she moved into the fair, but spots of rain were starting to fall.

"Fucking marvellous!" Harry said. "This rain will fucking ruin my outfit!"

"Mine too!" Crystal said as she made her way around the back of the big top and entered Mr. Tickles' tent. The smell of incense immediately replaced that of the disgustingly mixed odours of the fairground. It was much darker inside the tent, as only a candle here and there flickered. A cold rain-laden wind blew through the opening to the tent, giving Crystal a chill. Gooseflesh prickled her arms.

"Hello?!"

In the distance, a bird screeched and beat its wings in alarm. "Intruder, intruder, intruder!" the bird yapped.

"What the fuck is that squawking all about?!" Harry bellowed.

"Who's there?!" came a heavy voice. "Answer me, or you'll feel the sharp side of my sword!"

"It's Crystal!" she said.

"Who's the man that's with you?"

"It's Harry!"

"I thought you said he was just a puppet?"

"He is!" Crystal protested, stepping back against the tent's entrance.

"Show yourself, woman. *Now*!"

Crystal stepped out of the gloom and revealed her tightly wrapped body – the dragon dress had been a perfect choice for her voluptuous figure. She looked directly at Mr. Tickles, who stood at the other end of the tent with his women either side of him. As promised, he had a sword in hand. A Samurai, which made Crystal shudder.

I wouldn't want a poke with that thing! she thought, eyeing the clown and his deadly duo. The female clown, Miss Sideshow Necrotic, stood slightly behind her master and held a hammer so big, it looked as though it belonged in a comic book.

The other one, Miss Sideshow Nightshade, AKA Parris, was also in full view. She too had a collar around her neck, with a thick length of chain attached to it. Unlike Sideshow Necrotic, Sideshow Nightshade had an eight-inch Bowie knife in her hand, with another strapped to her hip. Also unlike her colleagues, she didn't wear a jester or clown outfit – she still had on her black busted jeans, patched leather jacket and biker boots.

"*Phwoar*!" Harry growled. "Dark meat, and she looks good enough to eat!"

Sideshow Nightshade bared her sharp teeth and hissed at Harry and Crystal.

"Harry!" Crystal barked. "You'll have to excuse him, he gets rather excited around new people and er, em…women…" She let herself trail off, worried she was sounding like an idiot.

"I can't help thinking she's a tasty bit of arse!" Harry said, then boomed with laughter. "The other one ain't too shabby, either."

"Harry!"

"However, I don't fancy yours much!" he said, then started laughing again.

"I am so, so sorry!" Crystal said. "He's such a rude boy!"

The atmosphere inside the tent felt heavy after Crystal stopped speaking – the only sound came from the rattle of the chains that bound the ladies to their master.

Crystal gulped.

"Whose fucking mother died?!" Harry asked.

"Ha—"

"Shut it, bitch, and light me a cigar!"

Obeying Harry, Crystal lit a cigar and placed it in Harry's mouth.

"Now, are we going to stand around here all night, bitches, or are we going to rock'n'roll?!"

"Bah-ha-ha-ha!" Mr. Tickles bellowed, bending over and smacking one of his massive thighs with his overzealousness. "Bloody brilliant!" he said, starting to applaud. This set off the two women, who started to titter and point, causing Crystal to join in.

"You fucks find me funny? Do I look like a goddamn clown to you lot? Do I?!"

"You're very good, Crystal," Mr. Tickles said. "I didn't see your mouth moving at all!"

"The light is poor in here, master..." Sideshow Necrotic ribbed.

Mr. Tickles yanked on her chain. "Silence, you insolent swine! They are our guests!" he barked.

Sideshow Nightshade smiled and licked her lips on seeing her colleague in pain and discomfort. "Mmm," she said, snaking her hands down her body in a sexual and sensual way.

"Don't be afraid, Crystal. Step forward," the huge clown said. "You're in safe company here."

Moving forward with confidence, Crystal stood before Mr. Tickles and his Sideshow counterparts. "You seem nervy on this encounter, Mr. Tickles – did my entrance alarm you?" she asked him.

He narrowed his eyes as if to say 'You dare call me a coward?' "What would make you say such a thing?" he asked. "Do I seem nervous?"

"You just don't seem yourself. It's hard to explain."

A shadow cast over her as he stepped up to her, his chest in her face.

Harry and Crystal both looked up at the monster of a man and smiled – flickers of light danced across his freaky make-up. When he smiled, he exposed sharp, yellow teeth, but not all of them were intact – some were chipped and scuffed.

A growl rose from his stomach and brought with it a gust of foul-smelling breath. A hint of whiskey could be detected, along with a vile odour of stale blood and sweat.

Will you walk into my parlour, said the spider to the fly…

"Hey, fatty – do you need to stand so fucking close?!" Harry asked, prodding Mr. Tickles in his protruding gut.

"Your lips didn't move. No gulp or movement of the throat."

Crystal flushed. "I know…" is all she said.

"What's the deal with that doll?" he asked her as he swayed the chains to his showgirls lightly.

"Harry's real," she said. "I don't need to talk for him, as he can talk for himself."

A rapture of laughter burst from behind Mr. Tickles. "*Silence!*" he yelled, making Crystal quiver. His voice was as big as his frame. Somewhere in the distance, Crystal could hear people cheering and laughing – roller coasters whooshed and zoomed along their tracks, causing a cacophony of loud clattering sounds.

"Are you all there in the head?" he asked.

Crystal nodded. "Of course. If people believed, then my act would be worthless." He raised his hands as if expecting her to hand Harry over, causing Crystal to pull back. "Nobody gets to touch or hold him."

"Back off, fat boy!" Harry said. "I have weapons, and I ain't afraid to use them!"

Mr. Tickles snorted out a laugh. "Alive or not, I love it! Maybe you'd consider joining my crew once this is over?"

"So we can shovel elephant shit for the rest of our careers?!" Harry said.

Mr. Tickles lost his smile. "You'd finally fulfil that dream of yours, Crystal. We travel the world. You'd see some of the big cites: L.A, New York, London, Tokyo, Paris…We go everywhere. You'd never have to worry about work, fame and money ever again. And as far as being hunted by the police? You'd never have to worry about that, either – the circus would protect you like a family protects its own…"

He turned his back on her and started to walk away.

"Would you put me on a chain like a dog?" she asked. "Just like that pair?!"

"No – you would be the star of your own show. I'm well in with the ringmaster, who is always looking to recruit new material."

"I don't know…"

"Think about it. The circus doesn't pull out of here until tomorrow night."

"Okay, I'll think it over."

He nodded. "And you were right, I am a little nervous."

"Why?" she asked.

He told her about the surprise visit from his brother, and how he thinks he's Father Christmas' evil twin brother, and that every day and preceding day is Christmas Eve and Christmas Day to him. That he's stuck in a deranged fantasy loop.

"Santa Klaws…" Harry uttered. "Klaws spelt K L A W S."

Mr. Tickles looked at them. "You know about him?"

"Yes, from that book – *White Walls*."

"Oh, yes, of course – I'd forgotten about his appearance in that. It would seem that Wadsworth is gathering us…"

"He's the author of the book!" Crystal blurted.

Mr. Tickles' mouth flopped open. "My God, you're probably right!"

"He's gathering us to tell us that – to reveal how and why he did it."

"Yes! Come on, we should get to his place or we're going to be late."

"Will you join me in my van? There's plenty of room for all three of you," she said.

The clown nodded. "Lead the way," he said, then pulled on the chains, causing both Sideshows to follow him.

When they stepped out of Mr. Tickles' tent, they noticed the rain had stopped, much to Crystal's relief. I hate sitting around in wet clothes, she thought.

As they walked forward, an awe-inspiring scene unfolded before Crystal's and Harry's eyes – a hush fell over the crowd, which parted like the Red Sea, with Mr. Tickles and Co. acting as their Moses.

"Get the fuck out of my face!" the clown barked as people came close to take snaps with their cameras and phones – a few were snatched from their owners and stomped on. When they protested, Mr. Tickles and the Sideshows either shoved them out of the way or snarled in their direction.

"That's it, cunts! Get out of the fucking way," Harry said, and then laughed.

Crystal could do nothing but smile as they passed through the crowd and to the main gates of the fairground with ease. As they headed toward the car park, they passed the Cabin Bar, where a few drunks had gathered.

"Hey, Ronald McDonald!" one of them yelled. His speech was slurred. Crystal watched as Mr. Tickles turned to face the bald-headed man, who was covered in tattoos – "New Breed Skinheads" was etched on his neck. His arms and legs looked stick-thin, which matched his skinny torso. Chains dangled from his black, holey jeans.

"Yeah?" Mr. Tickles asked, getting closer to the man.

Three of the skinhead's goons got up from the bench they were sat at and stood behind their fearless leader.

Crystal stepped back and out of the way.

"This should be interesting!" Harry said.

"Maybe we should get to the van?" Crystal said.

"Not a fucking chance – I want to see this!"

"Oh, we've got one with a set of nuts here, boys," Skinhead said, causing his drunken buffoons to laugh hysterically – they reminded Crystal of a strung-out cackle of hyenas, which made her smile.

"Yeah, fucking looks like it, too!" the biggest of the bunch said. He had weasel-like eyes, with a huge Swastika tattooed on his throat. Like his brethren, he too had "New Breed Skinheads" stencilled on his neck. "I say we fucking do him!" Swastika said.

"Make your move, ladies!" Mr. Tickles said, and then shoved Skinhead so hard that he pushed through his three mates and crashed against a load of tables and chairs.

"What the fuck?!" Swastika said.

As he was about to take a swing, both Sideshows were on him. Nightshade bit into the guy's neck whilst Necrotic went for his eyes with one hand and his tongue with the other.

The two other skinheads were having none of it, as they ran off.

Crystal walked over to the fallen skinhead and then kicked him in his throat as he tried to get up. He collapsed back to the floor and gagged, which highly amused both Crystal and Harry.

"Whoa, ladies. Whoa!" Mr. Tickles called as he pulled both Sideshows off Swastika. Once they were free of him, nothing could be seen of the man's face – it dripped with blood. Part of his left ear had either been bitten or torn off, with his neck a blood-soaked mess. The women had clearly punched and kicked him, as both of his eyes were closed to slits.

As they left the scene, people rushed over to help. Nightshade looked back over her shoulder at Swastika. "Make sure you stay out of the sun, dickhead, or you'll likely wind up with a hell of a tan!" she said, then laughed.

After crossing the road and entering the car park, Crystal noticed the limo was still sat between the recycling bins. She eyed it with curiosity, as this time it was rocking on its chassis.

What on earth is going on inside that thing? she wondered, unable to rip her gaze from it.

"Are you going to open the van, woman?" Harry asked, but Crystal ignored him. "Hey, gal – wake up!" he yelled, snapping her out of her glazed-over state.

"Huh?" she asked.

"The van, dopey. Open up! We're freezing our asses off here!" Harry snapped.

"But you've got a wooden arse, Harry!" Nightshade said.

"And? It still gets fucking cold!"

Nightshade laughed, and so did Mr. Tickles as they got into the back of the van. Once they were loaded in, Crystal started her vehicle and drove out of the parking area. "Do you know where this mansion is?" she asked the three in the back.

"Yeah," Mr. Tickles said. "I used to know someone who lived close to it. Just keep going – I'll guide you."

When Mr. Tickles started to lead them out of town and away from Porthcawl, Crystal thought the clown was wrong. "Are you sure this is right?"

"Yes, definitely," he said.

"We seem to be moving out of town, though."

"I know."

"Doesn't the mansion come under Porthcawl?" she asked.

"Yes, but it's on the outskirts," he advised. "Take your next left."

Following his instructions, Crystal found herself on a narrow road which looked like an old B-road. As she was about to ask if this was the right way again, she saw a signpost which indicated the location of the mansion; on seeing the sign, her nerves eased.

At least I know he's not leading me off somewhere to kill me, she thought.

The rest of the journey up to the mansion was quiet – nobody spoke.

When they got to the gate, Crystal pressed the buzzer.

"Yes?" came a voice.

"Hi, is this Wadsworth?"

"Is this Crystal?"

"Yes," she said.

"Please, come on up to the house. "

"But—" she continued, but the intercom went dead. Before her, the gates opened. She drove through.

On the grounds to the mansion, Crystal was in awe at the size of the building and surrounding area – it was comprised of four floors, conservatories on either side, fountains, two garages, stables and woodland at its rear.

"Jesus, what a piece of property!" Crystal uttered.

"One day, this is how we'll be living, baby."

"I'd like to think so, Harry, I really would."

"If you decide to come and work for us," Mr. Tickles said, "then you won't need to worry about money ever again – you'd be paid very well for your skills, my dear."

"I'm thinking about it, don't you worry about that!" she said.

"Don't you think we should be getting in there?" Harry said. "The fucking suspense is killing me!"

"In a minute, Harry, please."

"My dear, if you are worried about your sister, don't be. I have your back, and so do my assistants," Mr. Tickles said.

"Oh, you've got enough to worry about, what with your brother who thinks it's Christmas Eve!" she said.

Both Sideshow Necrotic and Nightshade laughed, causing the giant clown to snarl in their direction. They immediately piped down. "What's so funny? Do I need to yank your chains?" he asked. Silence. "Good."

"We have your back though, Crystal," one of the women said. "Even if we do have our hands full with Klaws."

"Thanks," Crystal said, staring at the house. "I guess we should head in, hey?"

"Uh-huh!" Mr. Tickles grunted. "I'm sure no harm will come to any of us."

Crystal snorted. "Let's hope you're right, amigo," she said, getting out of the van and going around to Harry's side to help him out. Once he was snug in the crux of her arm, she went to the back of the vehicle and let Mr. Tickles and his women out. The van bounced on its chassis as the mass of weight disembarked.

"At least it's stopped raining!" he said, letting out a laugh and honking his imaginary clown nose.

Crystal and Harry just looked at him, unsure how to take his personality. "Okay, let's go – fancy leading the charge?" she asked Mr. Tickles.

"Yeah," he said, face sullen.

Walking past them with his two women in tow, Mr. Tickles approached the front door to the mansion and rang the bell without hesitation. Necrotic drew a hatchet from behind her back whilst Nightshade unsheathed her Bowie knife.

Crystal stood behind them all and pulled her butcher knife out of her purse – whatever rushed them, they'd need to go through the clown and his entourage first, she thought.

Harry also readied himself, grabbing one of his throwing stars.

Footfalls approached the door.

The doorknob turned with immense sluggishness, which only helped to heighten the tension.

"Easy does it…" Mr. Tickles said. "Easy…We don't want to go harming an innocent…"

"Fuck the innocents!" Harry said. "I ain't getting my arse killed through sloppiness."

The door flew open.

A skinny man in a butler suit stood before them, with two burly blokes at his back – they looked like FBI agents, with their black clothes, white shirts and dark shades. They even wore the same style of shoe.

"Ah, welcome! Do come in!" he said with a huge, silly grin on his face. "I'm Wadsworth."

They were hesitant to step forward.

"Please, come, come!" But still the guests didn't move – they just eyed the two men standing behind Wadsworth, which the butler picked up on. "Oh, I see – have my guards put you off?" he asked them.

"What's with the gorillas?" Mr. Tickles asked, not liking the cut of their jib.

"You'll have to excuse Olaf and Rotwiler – they are merely here for my protection," he said with a glint in his eye. "It also means you won't need all those sharp-looking things in here!"

"What the fuck is going on here, pal?!" Mr. Tickles said, grabbing Wadsworth by the lapels of his jacket and drawing him to his chest.

Rotwiler and Olaf went to intervene, but Wadsworth called them off.

"*My*! There's no need for violence, my good man. I can assure you, I mean you no—"

"Either you start talking, or I'm going to rip your guts out with my bare hands!"

"Please! Release me at once, or I shall set my guards on you – they are armed with guns, and will easily cut you down, sir."

"Do as he says!" Crystal said.

"Not until he starts talking!"

"All will be revealed once you're—"

"What's my brother doing in town?!"

"I—" Wadsworth was about to explain, but Mr. Tickles started to shake the butler in a violent way.

"Talk, damn it!"

"Please! Take your hands off me, sir. All will be explained inside – that's if you can adhere to my rules, of course."

"What's that supposed to mean?!" Crystal asked.

"If you don't play by my rules, then none of you will know the truth!"

At that moment, they all heard the click of a hammer as one of the bodyguards drew his gun. "Step away from my boss!" the man said. A massive scar ran from his temple to his jawline. *"Now!"* he barked, stepping closer to Wadsworth's shoulder.

Reluctantly, Mr. Tickles let go of the butler, and then smoothed his uniform back into place. "Okay, Smiler – you got it," he said, stepping away.

"Now, please, give your weapons to my...*associates* – you will not need them, I promise you."

Slowly, they all did as Wadsworth asked and handed them to the butch bodyguards, who remained at the butler's side.

"Is my sister here?"

Wadsworth poked his head around Mr. Tickles' frame and addressed Crystal. "Yes, my dear. But don't worry, she has been instructed not to harm you – a weapon was removed from her and given to my men."

Mr. Tickles was first through the door, stating he had no weapons, but still the guards patted him down.

He was followed by Sideshow Necrotic, who handed over her hatchet before being searched for further weapons.

"Thank you!" Wadsworth said.

Next over the threshold was Sideshow Nightshade, who handed over her Bowie knives, before Crystal stepped up and gave Smiler her butcher knife.

"And does the little fella have any—"

"Hey, *douche*, less of the 'little.' And no, he doesn't have anything on him!" Harry said to the guard, who growled and bared his teeth.

"Okay," Wadsworth said, chuckling and holding his hands up in mock terror. "If you'd all like to follow me, please." Turning his back on them, Wadsworth directed them all to the lounge and opened the door. "If you'd care to step inside and help yourself to a drink," he said, "proceedings will start as soon as our last guest arrives."

When the door was thrown wide, Crystal's and Sam's eyes immediately locked together.

"*You!*" Crystal saw her sister mouth. "I'm going to kill you!" Samantha raged, throwing her half-empty glass of wine to one side.

As she crashed across the room, Mr. Tickles stepped in front of Crystal, blocking Sam from getting to her.

"I'll kill you!" she raged as she fought against the unmovable mass of Mr. Tickles. "Get the fuck out of my..." she started, but her words trailed off when he grabbed her by her arms and pushed her from his body.

Holding her firm with his immense grip, Mr. Tickles smiled his sharp-toothed grin and fixed her with his bloodshot eyes. "Let's all try to play nice, is it?" he said in a low, eerie voice. "I'd hate to have to snap your neck, bitch!"

She shrank away as she tried pulling her arms free. "Please, let me go!" Sam begged.

"Do you promise to behave? Your sister will not harm you, if you do not make an attempt at her."

"You expect me to believe that?!" she spat.

"It's the truth, Sam!" Crystal said. "I didn't come here to hurt you – I just want to know what this whole fucked up situation is about!"

"I'll make a deal with you here and now – for tonight only, we make a truce. But, once this evening is over and we are out of here, it's back on between you and me!"

"I can live with that," Crystal said, and offered her hand, which Sam shook.

"Am I safe to let you go, Sam?" Mr. Tickles asked.

"Yes, of course. I always keep my word."

"For what it's worth, you look beautiful," Crystal said, wiping a tear from her eye.

"Fit as fuck, I'd say!" Harry chirped in.

"Who are you people?" Norm butted in. "Are you friends of Angharad?"

"Don't be a dipshit, Norm!"

Crystal looked at the man standing behind a wheelchair – which was holding a skeleton. Is he talking to himself? she thought. "Are you feeling all right?" she asked.

"Perfectly fine!" he said. "Why shouldn't I be?"

"Ignore that tart, Norm – or are you taken by her body?"

"No, Angharad – I have eyes only for you, and you know that. I only went with those other women so I could help fix you," he said.

A silence fell in the room.

Crystal looked at the other guests – their reactions mirrored one another, apart from Mr. Tickles, who walked up to Norm.

"You do know you're pushing a bag of bones around there, son, don't you?!" he asked, and then laughed hysterically, causing the Sideshows to join in.

"I don't think it's nice, you laughing at my wife. She doesn't like being laughed at!" Norm shouted, his face solid with seriousness. Stepping from behind the wheelchair, he pressed his body against Mr. Tickles'. He may have been shorter than the clown, but Norm looked very chiseled, his jaw square. "Now, if you'll apologise like I know you're going to, I'm sure this whole matter can be forgotten."

"Bah-ha-ha-ha!" Mr. Tickles bellowed in Norm's face. "You're fucked in the head, man! I'm not saying sorry for Jack shit." He gave Norm a slight push and turned his back on the man, who reminded Crystal of a stone.

"Well, Daisy? Are you just going to stand there like a little girl wetting yourself, or are you going to be a man and do something about that overweight KoKo?!"

Putting his hand on Mr. Tickles' shoulder, Norm turned the clown around and punched him in the face with his free hand. Mr. Tickles head flew to one side but the rest of him didn't move – a growl gathered in the pit of his stomach as a trickle of blood ran down his mouth.

He licked it away as he stepped closer to Norm and looked down on him. "Is that all you've got, Nancy?!"

Norm swung for the clown again, only to have his fist be caught in mid-air by Mr. Tickles' huge open hand. It closed around Norm's and squeezed. Clicking sounds ensued as Mr. Tickles compressed as hard as he could.

"Ah, get off! You're breaking my hand!" Norm whimpered.

The clown smiled – his teeth were covered in blood.

It took Olaf and Rotwiler to pull Mr. Tickles free of Norm, who crashed down onto the coffee table, which obliterated under his weight. He held his hand as he rolled about by Angharad's feet.

"Fucking pathetic!"

"I suggest you stay down," Mr. Tickles growled, "or you'll get a pasting!"

The bodyguards struggled to hold him back as Wadsworth stepped into the room.

"*Stop!*" Wadsworth yelled. "What the bloody hell is going on in here?! I asked for no violence! You have nothing against each other."

"That's a laugh!" Sam said.

Crystal gave her a hard stare. "You promised!" she said, knowing she couldn't fully trust her sister – she had to end her life, one way or another.

Sam nodded, and then looked away.

"You've broken the bloody table!" Wadsworth said. "That was brought back from the deepest parts of Congo!"

"It's a fucking coffee table!" Mr. Tickles said.

"God! I can't leave you lot unattended – could you all move into the dining area, please, before anything else is smashed? There you will find your first clue as to why you have all been gathered here this evening," Wadsworth said, ushering them out of the room.

"Aren't you coming?" Crystal asked the butler.

"Yes, of course," he replied sharply, before taking another disgusted look at the demolished table. He rolled his eyes and said, "Bloody commoners!"

"You got that right, doc!" Harry said. "Now can we please get this fucking freak show on the road? I'm getting splinters in my arse from all the waiting!"

"Harry!" Crystal said, then followed after the others.

"You two, with me!" Wadsworth instructed the guards before closing the doors to the lounge and following the guests to the dinning room.

THE DINNER

As they crowded around the massive dining table, which held ten guests and a seat at the head of the table for the master of the house, they all looked down at the printouts, which consisted of official documents, patient records and newspaper clippings.

"What the hell are these?" someone asked.

"No idea, but it looks weird," answered someone else as a hubbub of voices started to grow in the room.

"Please, please!" Wadsworth said, entering the room with his guards at his back. "If you could all find your place name and sit, that would be most marvellous!"

"Just what the hell is going on?!" Crystal asked.

"Yeah, what's the big idea, Jeeves?" Harry asked.

A few titters erupted around the room.

"If you all sit, you'll find out – you all have a print, which is a clue to why you are all here. Dinner will be served shortly," he said. "Now please, sit."

"Are you our host?" Norm asked.

"No – the host will be along after dinner. Your host is the main reason for you being here."

"Aren't we a guest short?" Sideshow Nightshade asked.

"Yes, Mr. Klaws," Wadsworth said. "He should have been here by now, which is most disturbing. I just hope he hasn't decided to run off into the night!"

"Well, he does think it's Christmas Eve!" Mr. Tickles said. "He's probably out delivering presents."

"Whatever do you mean?" Sam asked.

"Please, sit down and read your printouts – it will give you all an idea of what is going on!"

As they took their seats, they all started to thumb through the sheets of paper. One of the articles caught Crystal's and Harry's attention, which sent them into hysterics.

Experimentation and Escape: My Theory of the Castell Hirwaun Incident

Blog Post
by
Kindra Sowder

We've all heard about the three lunatics that have escaped from Castell Hirwaun: Norm Jenkins, Samantha Saunders, and "Santa Klaws" (true name unknown). There has been an outcry from the public about our safety and the lack of information given by news media, as shown by the following:

"Help me!!! Anyone know anything of the hirwaun hospital break out?!!! Need to know where to go and who to contact if I see anything that looks out of order."
Ian Guliford – Facebook

"Wtf! Did you hear about the escaped loonies? It bites that I had to hear it from the guy down the street and NOT from the news? Oh sure they mentioned it real quick but no details? Who are these people that are wandering around Hirwaun? Can kids play safely outside?"
Nicole Platania – Facebook

"Some psychos have apparently got out of the local nut house. Does this mean that it would OK if I answered the door to the next person who knocks by slammin them with a baseball bat?" Welcome to Hirwaun: where the old biddies who stick their nose into everyone's business are the safe ones because at least you know how dangerous they are"
Catz Davies – Facebook

One citizen even felt they would show their concerns with a small joke. I found it funny, but with so much fear in the community, how many would take it that way? Probably just trying to break the tension.

"OMG the lunatics have left the building... lock your doors and windows and hide your underwear...!"
Lynda Nashelle – Twitter

While I am just as concerned as anyone else at this point, the lack of information that has been divulged to us has everyone on edge. All we know is that these people are out and about and nothing else, but why? What are they covering up? One citizen voices her opinion with this post:

"What kind of idiots just loose three dangerous nut jobs? Why are we even keeping these psychos alive for that matter? My taxes paying for someone who could kill a bunch of people to have a free place to stay and be fed? Madness. Just euthanize the lot like you would to a dangerous dog!"

Sarah Fisher – via Facebook

She raises some great questions here. As we all know, the government has a tendency to do things we are unaware of, leaving us to speculate on their motives. This is no different. While euthanasia would probably be a great idea as far as the criminally insane that can't be treated are concerned, I believe the doctors over there at Castell Hirwaun have other ideas. What are they?

It's quite simple. These doctors are responsible for treating these patients and it has been proven throughout history that there are the rare doctors that have ulterior motives to "better" treatment methods. How do they do this? Experimentation on the people that trust them. This moves into my theory.

I have thought about this long and hard after seeing the very brief news bulletin about their so-called "escape." These individuals could very well be dangerous; possibly even killers for all we know. I believe the doctors over at Castell Hirwaun decided to experiment on these three, who are undoubtedly suffering from an array of mental illness, to see how it would affect them and their mental state. It has also been said you can only get true results outside of a clinical setting, which is why sometimes there have been experiments based on observed data where the subject has no idea they are being studied.

The only way for this to happen is for the doctors to set them loose, stand back, and watch as chaos unfolds. I'm not sure how they would've expected the public to react, but I cannot think of any other motive besides this.

I only have a few words of advice for our citizens: Lock your doors, don't go out unless you have to (especially after dark), and don't answer the door for anyone. Let's hope things don't get too crazy before the doctors decide to reel their subjects back in.

Other Information On the Reactions to Leaked News of a
'Possible' Escape at Castell Hirwaun. It would appear some are taking it with a pinch of salt:

"Just heard there's a load of mentalists on the loose in Hirwaun. This place is full of mentalists on an average day, so they should fit in quite well...

...provided they can all see off a can of Stella in under five seconds and have an affinity for wanking in the park!"

Martyn Grant – Facebook

"Hirwaun crazys running wild they can just join the fucking rest of us lets get out there and buy those nutters a drink. Already got me and the boys together for a few drinks to see if we can meet up with them, Hey anyone know what these guys look like and if Santa Klaws is not in a big red suit my night will be ruined #PissupinHirwaun"

Scott Holmes - Facebook

"Ok, I thought I'd seen it all on this bus. I was so wrong. Some dude dressed like a freak show Santa Claus just hopped on. I actually bailed out before my regular stop and walked the rest of the way to work in the rain, he wigged me out THAT bad. Is there some kind of mad circus in town I haven't heard about? *shudders*"

Sarah Dale – Facebook

"I've just heard a buzz saw in my attic followed by trademark lunatic escaping from the asylum giggling. I think I'm in serious trouble here..you'd better come quickly before they.... Oh. Holy hell-"

Rose Garnett – A captured 999 Call (Unclear What Happened).

"Don't understand how you can just 'lose' three people in this day and age. Can I hear you say 'conspiracy theory'???

Why has Facebook got more info on these escaped loony bin inmates than the local news station? I'm genuinely getting worried here and no one with any authority seems to be able to tell me anything! Nothing seems to be getting done either; no extra police around, no advice or support, and no extra safety precautions! Are we all supposed to just sit here and let our little community become invaded by these psychos? Good to know I can trust in those supposed to keep me safe in an emergency...NOT!!!

Hirwaun mothers and fathers Does anyone know if the schools are remaining open? Are you still sending your kids to school? Has anyone heard anything? Really don't feel safe having the little ones out of the house when no one seems to be telling me anything. Grrr!

Thoughts are with those living near the escaped mental health patients #prayforhirwaun"

Danielle Bowen – Personal Blog

"Oh, that last one is a funny read!" Harry said. "Did you throw that one in for fun?"

Wadsworth smiled and nodded. "Yes, I thought it would lighten the mood."

"What the hell is the rest of it though, Harry?" Crystal asked her wooden companion, who sat in his own chair beside her.

"I have no idea, but that skeleton keeps winking at me!" he said.

"Harry! Keep your voice down."

"Are you talking about my wife?!" Norm asked, getting up from his chair.

This caused Mr. Tickles to stand up and ready himself in Crystal's defence. "Sit down, Norm, or I'll flatten you!" he said.

"Huh!" Norm huffed. "You got lucky, my friend, that's all that was in the other room!"

"Oh, you think so, do you?! My, we are feeling brave, aren't we!"

"Wait a minute!" Crystal raised her voice so she could be heard over the two men arguing. "I think I've cracked it!"

Norm and Mr. Tickles looked at her in surprise. "What are you talking about?" Norm asked.

"Yeah, sis!" Sam said, managing to make the word 'sis' sound scornful. "Why don't you tell us what this shit means?" She then threw her printout across the room.

"What have you cracked, your pussy?!" Harry asked, turning to look at her.

"He's so adorable!" Sideshow Necrotic said.

"So are your tits, honey!" he told her.

"Oh, you're a cheeky devil!" she said, giving Harry a wink.

"Don't you flirt with my man, bitch, or I'll gut you!" Crystal said, picking up a knife from the table.

Necrotic held her hands up in defence.

"Crystal, calm down!" Mr. Tickles said.

"Get your whore in line, then!" she warned him.

"*Norm, get me out of this place!*"

"I can't, Angharad, not until we know what's going on!" Norm said.

"Well, I was about to put a big piece of the puzzle together, until you lot started piping up!" Crystal said. "If you'd all just shut up for a second, I can explain."

"Yes, why don't you, Miss Saunders?" Wadsworth said, as he entered the room. "The others just want to fight, or so it would seem, and are totally oblivious to what is going on. But not you."

A hush fell over the room.

"Why have you brought us here, Wadsworth? Are you going to blackmail us – is that how you manage to keep such a fancy house?!"

"*Blackmail*? You must be mad! I've brought you here to help you all!" he said.

"*Help*?! Is that what you call it? I've been half-out of my mind with worry, and I'm sure the others have felt the same!"

"Why?"

"All this sneaking around and letters – it's pretty fucking cloak and dagger, don't you think? And a few of us are clearly in deep shit," she said, holding up her printout.

"What are you getting at, Crystal?" Mr. Tickles asked.

"I've already seen some of this crap, such as the patient files and newspaper clippings…" she said before tossing the sheets of paper across the room. "You should have too, Mr. Tickles!"

"Yes, I have, but what is it you think you know?" he pushed.

Before she answered, she turned to her sister. "Samantha, I want—I'm sorry."

"Crystal, what are you fucking doing?!" Harry asked.

"Oh, be quiet!" she snapped at him for the first time in their relationship. "From now on, I'm going to be the boss! And if you don't fucking like it, I'll throw you onto a fire and be done with it all!"

A gasp came from Harry and Samantha.

"But—"

"But nothing! Shut up and listen, wooden dick – the rest of you, too!"

"Wait until we get out of here, bitch!" Harry told her.

"Harry, please! Be quiet!"

"I—" Harry started, but Norm butted in.

"Tell us what you think you know?!"

"I don't *think* I know, I *do* know. I see the link in these sheets, as I know my sister and spent time with the clown. I'm surprised the rest of you can't see the link – it's right there in front of you!"

"Just spill!" Norm said.

"Yes, I agree!" said Mr. Tickles.

"Hang on!" she said. "I need to say something to my sister first." Looking at Sam, Crystal felt tears building in her eyes as her sister looked away from her. All the other guests looked at Crystal as she stood. "Sam, I have so much to say to you…"

"I wouldn't bother if I was you!" Sam said. "You'll put me off my food."

"You may not want to listen, but I'm going to tell you anyway."

"Just say what you have to say, so we can all find out what's going on and then go our separate ways!"

"*Huh*," Crystal sighed. "I want to make a confession."

"Bitch, be quiet – you have no idea—"

"Harry, love, I have to do this. The guilt has been weighing me down for far too many years. I thought I could cope with it all, but not any longer. All the running we have been doing, all the lies, all the killing, all the pretence of being an act...I can't take the strain," she said, tears running down her face.

"Crystal!" Harry bellowed. "I can't believe you are acting like this!"

"Shh, Harry," she said, stroking his face lovingly. "It's true, you know – you are the best thing that ever happened to me. I love you, but I need to get this weight off my chest."

Sam turned her head and looked at her sister – their eyes fused. "Just say what you have to," she said.

Crystal nodded. "My sister is innocent of her crimes. It was me who committed the murders."

"What murders are you talking about?" Mr. Tickles asked.

"My parents – I killed them, and blamed it all on her. I've regretted it for years, and I'm truly sorry, Sam." More tears rolled down Crystal's face. "I know you'll never be able to forgive me, and I know you want to take my life, but I just wanted you to know that I'm sorry. I've always loved my baby sister, and I'm deeply sorry for what I did to you..."

Sam wiped a few loose tears from her face but said nothing.

"And if I need to tell this all to the police, then I will – I won't see you going back to that hospital, Sam."

"Why did you do it?!" Sam asked.

"Because I was jealous of you – you had it all. You even had Mam and Dad's approval of everything. They didn't even want me going to drama school or anything – they had me trapped. I felt suffocated. They needed to be removed from my life, which Harry helped me to see. I saw you as my scapegoat, I'm sorry," she said, wiping tears away. "That day at the hospital, I planned to break you out…"

"*What*?!" Harry blurted. "I never knew that!"

"No, because I knew you'd be mad. That's why I wanted to go there that day, but you were so irate when you saw me, Sam, that I knew there was no way I could do it, and so I was forced to leave you there."

Sam stood there, her mouth open but no words coming out. "Did you plan to leave me there to rot?"

"No, I would have come back for you, but the time had to be right. You have to believe me!" Crystal pleaded. "The last few days, all I've been able to think about is what I was going to say to you, and now it's here, all I can really say is sorry. Sorry for the whole fucking mess I've caused, and sorry for killing your parents."

"You mean *our* parents?"

"Biologically, yes, but they will never, ever be my parents. I swear I hated them from the moment I opened my eyes…"

Sam sighed. "It's all too much to take in, Crystal. You had me locked away for ten fucking years! Ten! I think it's going to take more than a few choice words and some tears to make me come around, sorry."

"Will you try? After this, we could try to move on – you could come with Harry and me?"

"Hold the fuck on," Harry said. "We've always been a double act, you know that!"

"Don't fret, Harry – I don't think I'd be interested in tagging along!" Sam said, sitting down.

"But…" Crystal said, wiping more tears away before giving up.

The others looked at each other, unsure what to say.

"What a lovely speech!" Wadsworth said, clapping his hands. "Do you have anything else to tell us, Crystal?"

"Oh, er…Yes," she said, sniffing. "I want to tell you all about the connection here," she said. "Samantha, I know you were broken out of that hospital by the aid of Wadsworth. I also know that you were there Norm, along with Santa Klaws, who is Mr. Tickles' brother. I also know you all, and what you've all done."

"How?" Norm said, slamming his hand down on the table as he stood up. His posh chair scraped along the uncarpeted flooring and toppled over.

"Because Harry and I have read about you – we knew you all long before we met this evening."

"That's not possible!" Norm said.

"Oh, it is!"

"How?!"

"Because all our lives have been written in a book – a book that's been made to look like a piece of fiction!"

"But—" Norm started.

"Fuck, now she's done it!" Harry muttered.

"What book?" someone called.

"This one!" Wadsworth said, and threw a copy of *White Walls and Straitjackets* down onto the table.

"It's all true," Mr. Tickles said. "I've also read it – my girls, too. And if you look in the back, your patient files are there!"

Norm reached for it and thumbed through the tatty copy as the other guests spoke among themselves.

Leaving the table, Crystal walked up to Wadsworth, who turned to face her. She kneed him in the balls and punched him in the face as he went down. "You piece of shit! Why would you write something like that – why?! Answer me, damn it!"

Some of the others gasped as Crystal yelled at him.

Wadsworth's bulldogs were on her, their Glock 9mms pointed at her head.

"No need for that!" he said, waving his men off. "Please…" he coughed…"Ugh…You've got…Ugh…" He wheezed as he tried to regain control over his breathing. "I think I'm going to be sick!" he said as Smiler helped his boss to his feet.

"If you don't start feeding us some answers, we're going to cut you into tiny pieces," she said, grabbing him by his bollocks. "And I'll start by ripping these off!"

"Remove your hand!" Smiler said. "Now!"

Mr. Tickles stood up and grabbed a knife from off the table.

"Sit," the second guard told him, "or I'll put a round through your fucking nose!"

"You've got it wrong!" Wadsworth said, his voice going high as she released his balls.

"What have I got wrong?!"

"*Phwoar*!" Harry said. "This shit is making me hot!"

"I…I…" Wadsworth said, clutching his aching privates.

"Spit it out!" Crystal said.

"Yes, out with it!" Mr. Tickles said as he sat back down.

"We haven't got all night!" Norm chirped.

"I didn't write the book, damn it!" Wadsworth said, straightening.

"*What*?!" Crystal asked.

"If you'll allow me, please," he said. "Your host can explain much more than I can."

"Well, where the fuck is he or she?" Mr. Tickles asked.

"I shall go and get *him*," Wadsworth said. Before excusing himself, he told his men to watch them closely and they did, with their guns un-holstered.

Crystal remained where she was.

"I say we make a run for it whilst he's gone!" Norm said.

"And what about those two, you flamin' idiot?!"

"No, no! We may as well see it out to the end," Crystal said, and both Sideshows agreed. "I want to know what this fucking pantomime is all about!"

"Yeah…" Mr. Tickles started, but a squeaking sound behind Crystal grabbed his attention – hers, too, as she turned to look out into the hall.

Heading towards Crystal was Wadsworth – he was pushing a wheelchair. The person in the seat had a bag over their head. As Wadsworth entered the plush-looking dining area, he announced, "And here is your host!" before whipping the bag off the person's head.

When the face was revealed, nobody said anything.

"Who is he?" someone asked.

Crystal couldn't take her eyes off the large bearded man in the wheelchair. He wore glasses, which were misted over – his hair was long. His mouth had been gagged; she thought she knew him, yet had never met him.

"Who are you?" she asked him.

"Mmm-mmm!" he mouthed beneath the gag – he tried to move his hands and legs, but they were tied.

"Allow me," Wadsworth said, slipping the man's gag down. "I had to restrain him – he's most violent."

"Who the fuck are you?" Tickles asked the bound man, stepping closer.

"Did you write this thing?" Norm asked, getting up from the seat and hitting the man around the face with the book.

"*Ah*, you bastard!" the man said.

"Fucking answer him!" Crystal screamed.

They all crowded around the tied individual.

"Yes! Yes, I wrote the damn thing!"

"Who are you? How do you know so much about us?" Norm asked.

"Some of you were in Castell Hirwaun with me – don't you remember speaking to me? I guess the shock therapy can cause memory loss…"

"You were in there?!" Crystal asked.

"Yes," he said, lowering his head.

"What for?" Harry asked.

"I had a problem with sex!" he answered.

Crystal sniggered. "I didn't know they put you away for such things, dear?!"

Harry laughed.

"Well, that explains their stories, but what about me? Where did you get your information?" Mr. Tickles questioned.

"Your brother knows more than he is letting on. You'd be surprised what people say when they are drugged to their eyeballs!"

"What's your name?"

"David," Wheelchair-man said. "I won't part with my surname – it's not something any of you need to know."

"How did you know about Harry and me?" Crystal asked.

"Through talking to your sister – when I heard about the killing of critics, I went back to Castell Hirwaun and spoke to Sam. Of course, she was half out of her mind on drugs and said you'd most probably committed the crimes. I didn't intend to get anyone in trouble, I swear."

"Oh, is that right?" Mr. Tickles asked.

"Yes, I swear! I've always liked writing, and so after leaving the hospital – semi-cured, I may add – I was told to find something to do. So I took up writing. I had plenty of ideas after meeting Norm, Sam and Santa Klaws."

"You fucking idiot!" Mr. Tickles said. "Couldn't you have come up with something original? How clichéd – you wrote about an asylum and a bunch of lunatics. How original!"

"I never proclaimed to be Stephen King, you know! I discovered a raw talent and put it to use."

"We could sue your arse!" Harry said.

"Yes!" Norm agreed.

"Look, I didn't think the book would go anywhere! I showed it to a friend and the next thing I knew, it was printed!"

"Why let that happen?!" Crystal asked.

"The money, I guess. Not only that, I thought it would be pretty awesome to see something in print. Who wouldn't?!"

"Yeah, making money off the back of us, you bastard!" Norm said.

"Calling me names isn't going to help. Besides, I never knew you lot would cotton on – most of you were drugged up when I came into contact with you. I never thought you'd find out!"

"Well, we did!" Norm said.

"What in the fuck are we going to do with him?" Mr. Tickles asked Wadsworth.

"Don't ask me. I'm just the butler, sir."

"And what do you do, exactly?" Norm asked.

"I buttle, sir."

"I'm sure your heavies could help us out!" Sam said, indicating the beefcakes.

"Maybe, but as far as I see it, this is your problem, not mine. You can just wheel him out of here and do as you wish," he said. "I've done my part."

"A fat lot of good you've been!" Sideshow Necrotic said.

"We need to try and get those books recalled!" Crystal said.

"I'm sure I could get that done, as long as you don't hurt me," David said. "Please, untie me!"

"Can't we have some fun with him?" Sideshow Necrotic said, sitting on his lap. "He seems *up* for a bit of fun!" Giggling, she gave David a slap across his face.

"Do with him as you wish," Wadsworth said. "I brought you all here to deal with him."

"Wait a minute!" Norm said. "How did you know about him?!"

"Why, that's simple – I own Castell Hirwaun. I know everything that goes on behind those walls. I have access to everything. A few years ago, I had all the rooms bugged, including the staff unit. I caught wind of this fella's intention and kept tabs on him ever since."

"How very noble of you!" Norm said.

"Thank you, sir."

"I was being—"

"Never mind the jokes," Mr. Tickles said. "There's something else we're forgetting here…"

Five hard knocks at the font door caused a hush to fall over the guests.

"Untie me!" David demanded. "I haven't done anything wrong!"

"Shh!" Crystal said.

"We overlooked Klaws!" Wadsworth said, looking through the open dining room door and out into the hall.

"Untie me, damn it!" David said. "I said I'd recall the books, what else do you want from me?!"

"Shh!" Wadsworth said.

Then there was silence, followed by another five hard knocks on the door, and then a faint "*Ho-ho-ho.*"

"Well, we'll have to let him in," Mr. Tickles said. "You invited him, after all, Wadsworth – he should know what's going on!"

Wadsworth cleared his throat before speaking. "Olaf, go and see who's at the door," he told his non-scarred bodyguard.

The man nodded, cocked his gun, and headed out the room.

Everyone in the dining room listened.

They firstly heard the clack of deadbolts, as the guard unlocked the main door, which was then followed by it being swiftly opened. "Are you—" the man said, but his words were cut short. A loud *thunk* and groan ensued, followed by a single gunshot.

"What the hell?!" Crystal said.

"*Fuck*! Untie me!" David said.

Crystal moved away from the wheelchair and stood by Mr. Tickles. "That didn't sound good!"

"I agree."

"Rotwiler!" Wadsworth said. "Go and help Olaf."

"Come on, Angharad, we're leaving."

"I'd advise you to stay with us," Mr. Tickles said.

The front door slammed shut, which echoed throughout the mansion. A squeaking sound followed.

"What in fuck's name?!" Harry said.

"Untie me, damn it!" David said. "*Please!*"

Crystal went to him and started to pick at the knots in the rope.

The squeaking sound became louder, closer.

Eeeeeeek-eeeeeeek

"What is...?" Mr. Tickles started saying, then stopped.

Crystal looked back at him. "What the..?!" she said, letting her words trail off, as she saw the butler making a run for it. "Stop!"

"Sorry, but you're all on your own!" he yelled back over his shoulder, laughing as he did so. In the distance, a couple of doors banged shut.

"Shit, he's gone!" Mr. Tickles said, stating the obvious before raising his hand slowly and pointing. "You may want to look out!" he said.

Turning to face the open door, Crystal saw a huge man dressed in a black Santa uniform. He stalked towards her, dragging the remains of Olaf behind him. A fire axe was planted in the dead man's head.

"Stop!" Rotwiler ordered, aiming his gun at Klaws' head as he walked towards the dinning room door.

When the huge Father Christmas got to the door, with blood now visible in his beard, he shouted, "Ho-ho-ho!" and then threw the body of Olaf in Rotwiler's direction. Olaf connected with the man and threw him off his feet. The gun slipped from his grip and slid under the table.

"No!" Rotwiler yelled as he tried to get the weight of Olaf off him. "Help!"

But all the others could do was get out of Klaws' way as he walked up to the fallen bodyguard and stamped on his head repeatedly. "Naughty, naughty, naughty, naughty…" He grunted over and over as he did so, until there was nothing but a lump of mush on the floor.

"Please. *Help*!" David said, managing to rip one hand free of the wheelchair.

Crystal moved clear and grabbed Harry. "We need to get out of here!" she said.

"I agree! Fuck everything else – this party's gone tits up!" Harry said.

Turning, Crystal saw Sideshow Necrotic and Nightshade lunge for Santa. Necrotic ended up caught in a bear hug. In one vicious squeeze, Santa broke her back and threw her to one side.

When she hit the floor, she didn't move.

"*Noooooooooo!*" Mr. Tickles yelled.

Before he could go for his brother, Crystal grabbed him by the arm. "We have to get the hell out of here. *Now!*"

Nodding, he let go of Nightshade's chain as she tore and bit Klaws.

"Shit!" Norm said, and ran for Angharad.

"Let's get the fuck out of here!" Harry said. "Out the window."

"*Argh!*" someone screamed.

Looking back, Crystal saw Klaws break Nightshade's neck before putting his massive hands either side of the writer's head – he tried crushing it like a grape, but somehow the writer managed to break free and dove under the table for the gun.

"*Move!*" Crystal screamed, watching Klaws close in on the writer as he scrabbled about for the gun – chairs were knocked over as he crawled.

As David got a hand to the weapon, Klaws dragged him from under the table and threw him against a wall. Paintings fell as the author crashed to the floor; blood trickled out of his mouth as he raised the gun and fired.

The first bullet zipped through the air and burst a few bulbs in the chandelier hanging above the dining table. The second and third shots buried themselves into a wall close to Crystal, who ducked out of the way.

Klaws gripped the writer's T-shirt, and ripped him off the floor and into a bear hug. With the little energy he had left, David managed to raise the gun once again, but before he could fire, Klaws squeezed his arms tight around him.

David's gun hand dropped, but not before a shot was fired – the slug punched into Klaws' shoulder. He growled and dropped his prey.

"Such a naughty child!" he said, grabbing the writer by his head and crushing it like a grape. The force was so strong, it caused an eyeball to pop free and push David's glasses off his face.

Knowing there was no hope for David, who bucked and thrashed in Klaws' grip, Crystal turned and watched as Mr. Tickles launched himself through the bay window, taking the blinds and curtains out into the cold, rainy night with him. When he disappeared, Crystal heard him grunt as he hit the floor.

"Come on!" she heard him call. "Jump down!"

Looking back over her shoulder, she saw Norm dash out of the room with Angharad, avoid a swipe from Klaws, and move into the hallway. There's nothing I can do for him, she realised.

Quickly scanning the floor, she noticed Nightshade's body had vanished…

"*Huh*?!" she gasped, but didn't have time to speculate.

She went to the window and was about to jump when Klaws grabbed her by her hair. She screamed as torrid pain tore through her scalp. Harry fell from her grasp and slid under the table after hitting the floor.

"You've been a bad, bad girl!" Klaws said, wrapping his hands around her throat. The dress she wore constricted her legs; she was unable to kick, knee or thrash.

"Lights out, bitch!"

"N…n…no!" Crystal choked out. "P…p…p…" she tried. Her arms flailed as she thrashed her body. When her right hand fell onto the table, she furiously searched for something – anything – that would get her out of danger. "Ha…Harry!"

Dark spots started to dance before her vision as her eyes rolled. This is it, she thought. I'm dead…

Then, as though some miracle had happened, Klaws' grip fell away and she crashed to the floor.

She took in a handful of deep breaths, trying to clear her vision. "Harry, you saved me!" she said from the floor, unable to turn. Putting her hands to her throat, Crystal tried rubbing the pain away, but it wasn't helping.

Regrouping, she got to her knees and saw that Harry was still under the table, unmoving and silent. She couldn't understand – why had he not helped? And who had? Turning, she saw Sam being crushed in a bear hug by Klaws as he tried to squeeze the life out of her.

"Sis?!" she gasped. "*You*?"

"Don't fucking stand there gawping at me – help!" she shouted, smashing a champagne bottle over Klaws' head. His grip on her broke, giving Crystal the chance to grab a chair and bash it over his back.

It didn't seem to have an effect on him, as he turned on Crystal and grabbed her by the throat.

"*Ugh!*" she gulped as he squeezed.

Before he could get a good hold, Sam plunged a shard of broken bottle into the side of his neck. He instantly let go of Crystal, who fell to the floor and grabbed Harry. With him snug in the crux of her left arm, she felt safe.

"Isn't that fat sack o'shit dead yet?!" Harry said.

"You could have helped me, Harry!"

"I was knocked out – it would have been a bit difficult. Anyway, I'm here now!" he said, then unleashed a fury of throwing stars into Klaws' back.

The big man growled as he staggered forward. Sam had to jump out of his way as he crashed into the wall behind her.

"He's finished!" Mr. Tickles said.

Crystal turned to see the clown standing in the room once again. He held in his hand a set of gardening shears. He opened and closed them repeatedly and rapidly as he spoke. "Come and fucking get yours, brother!"

He charged Klaws with the blades poking outwards. But before he could ram the steel home, the disturbed Father Christmas avoided his brother's attack and the gardening implement rammed into the wall.

"Let's go!" Crystal told Sam, picking a knife up off the table. Both women moved to the window as Klaws and Tickles engaged in a fight.

As Mr. Tickles tried to pull the shears from the wall, Klaws grabbed him by the front of his clown suit, pulled him in, and then head-butted him four times before pushing him backwards.

In his dazed state, Mr. Tickles collapsed to the floor, his nose broken. Blood pissed out of his nostrils, but he ignored it and tried to get back on his feet.

Moving in, Klaws kicked Tickles in his ribs, then punched him in the face. "I'm going to kill you slowly!" Klaws said, grabbing Mr. Tickles' ear. "And I'm going to enjoy it!"

"We'll see about that!" Tickles said, rolling onto his back and slamming a punch into Klaws' balls. As he bent over in agony, the clown bit down on the man's nose as hard as he could.

Bone snapped.

Blood spurted.

"*Argh*!" Klaws screamed, trying to push his brother off. "You fucking bastard!"

"You ain't fucking 'ho-ho-ho'ing now, ya fat bastard!" Tickles said, getting to his feet and raining blows into his brother's stomach. He finished with a mighty uppercut, which took the bad Santa off his feet.

He landed with a thunderous crash on top of the dinning table, which spilt and buckled under the weight.

"Kill me, will you?!" Tickles said, grabbing a table leg – his brother was leaking blood from all over. "I guess your killing days are over!"

He started to bludgeon his brother about the face and head, only stopping when his breath had run dry.

Klaws gargled as a fountain of blood popped from his sagging mouth.

"Let's get out of here!" Crystal said. "Come on, Tickles."

The clown leaped through the window first and crashed to the ground below. "Move!" he shouted up at them.

"I'm glad you managed to forgive me!" Crystal told Sam as she watched her move to the window.

"I'll never forget," Sam said with her back to Crystal.

Crystal pulled Sam backwards by her hair and exposed her throat. She placed the knife she'd picked up from the table to Sam's throat. "Sorry, sis, but I had to make it sound convincing – you didn't honestly think I'd let you walk out of here alive, did you?!"

"You fucking bitch!" Sam said, trying to wriggle free of Crystal's grip.

"I had to make sure I got your guard!" she said, pressing the knife tight against her sister's throat. "Sleep well…"

Sam managed an elbow to Crystal's guts, and spun around as the grip loosened. "I think you underestimated me, whore!" she said, cocking the gun Rotwiler had dropped and sticking it in Crystal's belly.

"Uh!" Crystal gasped as the hammer fell. Pain tore through her, and the blast

propelled her and Harry backward.

Before Crystal could move, her sister stood over her, the gun pointed at her face. "Like you, I too couldn't allow you to live, even if you meant the apology or not. I guess we're not that much different after all, Crystal," she said, cocking the weapon.

"Please…"

"Too…*Ugh!*" Sam gargled as a throwing star stuck in her neck. As she collapsed to one side, the gun went off, but the bullet went wide and ploughed into Klaws.

Managing to get to her feet, Crystal looked over her sister as she tried to stem the blood flow.

"What a sneaky fucking bitch!" Harry said. "It's a good thing I was prepared for her!"

"I'm sorry, Sam…" Crystal said, letting her words trail off as she jumped out the window.

Below, Mr. Tickles waited. He asked no questions, just helped her tighten a makeshift bandage around her gunshot.

THE AFTERMATH

With Klaws finished off, Crystal decided to join Mr. Tickles at his circus. And with Sideshow Necrotic dead, he needed a new act to replace her anyway. (Mysteriously, Sideshow Nightshade had been back at her cage, awaiting her master's return. When Crystal had said she'd seen the woman killed by Klaws, Nightshade had replied with, *"You can't kill what's already dead!"*

Out of respect, Mr. Tickles had taken time to bury Sideshow Necrotic on the grounds of the mansion. Once they had finished with that, they'd all piled into Crystal's van and headed back to Porthcawl. They'd half expected to see Norm or Wadsworth somewhere on the side of the road, but nothing was seen of them, which was probably a good thing, Crystal had thought.

"It would seem we are going to be one big happy family?" Crystal said.

"It would seem that way!" Mr. Tickles said.

"I guess we'll never know everything," Crystal said.

"Probably not," Mr. Tickles said.

"Wadsworth is still out there, and that could be a worry!"

"Does it fucking matter?" Harry asked. "We're out of that shithole. And as far as you being boss, Crystal, that isn't *ever* going to fucking happen!"

Again, they all laughed, and as the circus came into sight, they all felt safe, knowing the whole ordeal was over.

"You'll all be protected at the circus," Mr. Tickles said. "Trust me."

"I guess it's on to the next town!" Harry said. "When tomorrow rolls around, it'll be business as usual!"

The other two grunted in agreement.

"I'm looking forward to the adventures that lie ahead of us!" Crystal said.

"It's going to be fun, gang," Mr. Tickles said. "Just wait and see!"

The next evening, the circus pulled out of Porthcawl with Crystal and Harry in tow. As promised, Mr. Tickles had sorted it with his ringmaster, enabling them to become a part of his show.

Next stop, London.

After that, who knows?

Maybe a town near you…?!

OR DID IT END LIKE THIS...

A skinny man in a butler suit stood before them, with two burly blokes at his back – they looked like FBI agents, with their black clothes, white shirts and dark shades. They even wore the same style of shoe.

"Ah, welcome! Do come in!" he said with a huge, silly grin on his face. "I'm Wadsworth."

They were hesitant to step forward.

"Please, come, come!" But still the guests didn't move – they just eyed the two men standing behind Wadsworth, which the butler picked up on. "Oh, I see – have my guards put you off?" he asked them.

"What's with the gorillas?" Mr. Tickles asked, not liking the cut of their jib.

"You'll have to excuse Olaf and Rotwiler – they are merely here for my protection," he said with a glint in his eye. "It also means you won't need all those sharp-looking things in here!"

"What the fuck is going on here, pal?!" Mr. Tickles said, grabbing Wadsworth by the lapels of his jacket and drawing him to his chest.

Rotwiler and Olaf went to intervene, but Wadsworth called them off.

"*My*! There's no need for violence, my good man. I can assure you, I mean you no—"

"Either you start talking, or I'm going to rip your guts out with my bare hands!"

"Please! Release me at once, or I shall set my guards on you – they are armed with guns, and will easily cut you down, sir."

"Do as he says!" Crystal said.

"Not until he starts talking!"

"All will be revealed once you're—"

"What's my brother doing in town?!"

"I—" Wadsworth was about to explain, but Mr. Tickles started to shake the butler in a violent way.

"Talk, damn it!"

"Please! Take your hands off me, sir. All will be explained inside – that's if you can adhere to my rules, of course."

"What's that supposed to mean?!" Crystal asked.

"If you don't play by my rules, then none of you will know the truth!"

At that moment, they all heard the click of a hammer as one of the bodyguards drew his gun. "Step away from my boss!" the man said. A massive scar ran from his temple to his jaw line. *"Now!"* he barked, stepping closer to Wadsworth's shoulder.

Reluctantly, Mr. Tickles let go of the butler, and then smoothed his uniform back into place. "Okay, Smiler – you got it," he said, stepping away.

"Now, please, give your weapons to my…*associates* – you will not need them, I promise you."

Slowly, they all did as Wadsworth asked and handed them to the butch bodyguards, who remained at the butler's side.

"Is my sister here?"

Wadsworth poked his head around Mr. Tickles' frame and addressed Crystal. "Yes, my dear. But don't worry, she has been instructed not to harm you – a weapon was removed from her and given to my men."

Mr. Tickles was first through the door, stating he had no weapons, but still the guards patted him down.

He was followed by Sideshow Necrotic, who handed over her hatchet before being searched for further weapons.

"Thank you!" Wadsworth said.

Next over the threshold was Sideshow Nightshade, who handed over her Bowie knives, before Crystal stepped up and gave Smiler her butcher knife.

"And does the little fella have any—"

"Hey, *douche*, less of the 'little'. And no, he doesn't have anything on him!" Harry said to the guard, who growled and bared his teeth.

"Okay," Wadsworth said, chuckling and holding his hands up in mock terror. "If you'd all like to follow me, please." Turning his back on them, Wadsworth directed them all to the lounge and opened the door. "If you'd care to step inside and help yourself to a drink," he said, "proceedings will start as soon as our last guest arrives."

When the door was thrown wide, Crystal's and Sam's eyes immediately locked together.

"*You!*" Crystal saw her sister mouth. "I'm going to kill you!" Samantha raged, throwing her half-empty glass of wine to one side.

As she crashed across the room, Mr. Tickles stepped in front of Crystal, blocking Sam from getting to her.

"I'll kill you!" she raged as she fought against the unmovable mass of Mr. Tickles. "Get the fuck out of my…" she started, but let her words trailed off when he grabbed her by her arms and pushed her from his body.

Holding her firm with his immense grip, Mr. Tickles smiled his sharp-toothed grin and fixed her with his bloodshot eyes. "Let's all try to play nice, is it?" he said in a low, eerie voice. "I'd hate to have to snap your neck, bitch!"

She shrank away as she tried pulling her arms free. "Please, let me go!" Sam begged.

"Do you promise to behave? Your sister will not harm you, if you do not make an attempt at her."

"You expect me to believe that?!" she spat.

"It's the truth, Sam," Crystal said. "I didn't come here to hurt you – I just want to know what this whole fucked up situation is about!"

"I'll make a deal with you here and now – for tonight only, we make a truce. But once this evening is over and we are out of here, it's back on between you and me!"

"I can live with that," Crystal said, and offered her hand, which Sam shook.

"Am I safe to let you go, Sam?" Mr. Tickles asked.

"Yes, of course. I always keep my word."

"For what it's worth, you look beautiful," Crystal said, wiping a tear from her eye.

"Fit as fuck, I'd say!" Harry chirped in.

"Who are you people?" Norm butted in. "Are you friends of Angharad?"

"Don't be a dipshit, Norm!"

Crystal looked at the man standing behind a wheelchair – which was holding a skeleton. Is he talking to himself? she thought. "Are you feeling all right?" she asked.

"Perfectly fine!" he said. "Why shouldn't I be?"

"Ignore that tart, Norm – or are you taken by her body?"

"No, Angharad – I have eyes only for you, and you know that. I only went with those other women so I could help fix you," he said.

A silence fell in the room.

Crystal looked at the other guests – their reactions mirrored one another, apart from Mr. Tickles, who walked up to Norm.

"You do know you're pushing a bag of bones around there, son, don't you?!" he asked, and then laughed hysterically, causing the Sideshows to join in.

"I don't think it's nice, you laughing at my wife. She doesn't like being laughed at!" Norm shouted, his face solid with seriousness. Stepping from behind the wheelchair, he pressed his body against Mr. Tickles'. He may have been shorter than the clown, but Norm looked very chiseled, his jaw square. "Now, if you'll apologise like I know you're going to, I'm sure this whole matter can be forgotten!"

"Bah-ha-ha-ha!" Mr. Tickles bellowed in Norm's face. "You're fucked in the head, man! I'm not saying sorry for Jack shit." He gave Norm a slight push and turned his back on the man, who reminded Crystal of a stone.

"Well, Daisy? Are you just going to stand there like a little girl wetting yourself, or are you going to be a man and do something about that overweight KoKo?!"

Putting his hand on Mr. Tickles' shoulder, Norm turned the clown around and punched him in the face with his free hand. Mr. Tickles head flew to one side but the rest of him didn't move – a growl gathered in the pit of his stomach as a trickle of blood ran down his mouth.

He licked it away as he stepped closer to Norm and looked down on him. "Is that all you've got, Nancy?!"

Norm swung for the clown again, only to have his fist get caught in mid-air by Mr. Tickles' huge open hand. It closed around Norm's and squeezed. Clicking sounds ensued as Mr. Tickles compressed as hard as he could.

"Ah, get off! You're breaking my hand!" Norm whimpered.

The clown smiled – his teeth were covered in blood.

It took Olaf and Rotwiler to pull Mr. Tickles free of Norm, who crashed down onto the coffee table, which obliterated under his weight. He held his hand as he rolled about by Angharad's feet.

"Fucking pathetic!"

"I suggest you stay down," Mr. Tickles growled, "or you'll get a pasting!"

The bodyguards struggled to hold him back as Wadsworth stepped into the room.

"*Stop*!" Wadsworth yelled. "What the bloody hell is going on in here?! I asked for no violence! You have nothing against each other."

"That's a laugh!" Sam said.

Crystal gave her a hard stare. "You promised," she said, knowing she couldn't fully trust her sister – she had to end her life, one way or another.

Sam nodded, and then looked away.

"You've broken the bloody table!" Wadsworth said, "That was brought back from the deepest parts of Congo!"

"It's a fucking coffee table!" Mr. Tickles said.

"God! I can't leave you lot unattended!" he said sharply, before taking another disgusted look at the demolished table. He rolled his eyes and uttered, "Bloody commoners!" under his breath.

"What did you call us?" Mr. Tickles said.

"May I remind you of the hired hands, sir," Wadsworth said, indicating the FBI wannabes. "So, please, if you could all just take a seat so I can kick proceedings off…"

"What have you got in your hands?" Mr. Tickles asked.

"Please. *Sit*!" the butler demanded, losing his patience. "I have in my hands some interesting information which has come my way – it will help explain one or two things, I'm sure."

"Is it the newspaper clipping you sent me?" Crystal asked.

"No—well, yes, it's in here, among other clippings, documents, and records," Wadsworth said, giving each person in the room a printout.

"What the hell is this shit?!" Mr. Tickles asked. "I didn't come here to read, I came here to find out the truth!"

"If you take five minutes to read through that, it will give you some form of indication."

A hush fell over the room as the guests leafed through the papers Wadsworth had given them.

"*Ha*! I love the sheet of Facebook posts – they're fucking hilarious!" Crystal said.

"What's *Facebook*?" Norm asked.

Crystal looked at him. "Never mind, it'll take too long to explain."

"I see what's going on here," Sam said.

"What?" Crystal asked.

"Yes, spill!" Norm said.

"Care to enlighten the rest of the group, Samantha?" Wadsworth said.

"Yes, tell us, Sam!" Harry pushed.

"Well—"

Before she could say another word, Crystal broke in. "Samantha, I want—I'm sorry."

"Crystal, what are you fucking doing?!" Harry asked.

"Oh, be quiet!" she snapped at him for the first time in their relationship. "From now on, I'm going to be the boss! And if you don't fucking like it, I'll throw you onto a fire and be done with it all!"

A gasp came from Harry and Samantha.

"But—"

"But nothing! Shut up and listen, wooden dick – the rest of you, too!"

"Wait until we get out of here, bitch!" Harry told her.

"Harry, please! Be quiet! I need to say something to my sister." Looking at Sam, Crystal felt tears building in her eyes as her sister looked away from her. All the other guests looked at Crystal as she stood. "Sam, I have so much to say to you…"

"I wouldn't bother if I was you!" Sam said. "You'll put me off my food."

"You may not want to listen, but I'm going to tell you anyway."

"Just say what you have to say, so we can all find out what's going on and then go our separate ways!"

"*Huh*," Crystal sighed. "I want to make a confession."

"Bitch, be quiet – you have no idea—"

"Harry, love, I have to do this. The guilt has been weighing me down for far too many years. I thought I could cope with it all, but not any longer. All the running we have been doing, all the lies, all the killing, all the pretence of being an act…I can't take the strain;," she said, tears running down her face.

"Crystal!" Harry bellowed. "I can't believe you are acting like this!"

"Shh, Harry," she said, stroking his face lovingly. "It's true, you know – you are the best thing that ever happened to me. I love you, but I need to get this weight off my chest."

Sam turned her head and looked at her sister – their eyes fused. "Just say what you have to," she said.

Crystal nodded. "My sister is innocent of her crimes. It was me who committed the murders."

"What murders are you talking about?" Mr. Tickles asked.

"My parents – I killed them, and blamed it all on her. I've regretted it for years, and I'm truly sorry, Sam." More tears rolled down Crystal's face. "I know you'll never be able to forgive me, and I know you want to take my life, but I just wanted you to know that I'm sorry. I've always loved my baby sister, and I'm deeply sorry for what I did to you…"

Sam wiped a few loose tears from her face but said nothing.

"And if I need to tell this all to the police, then I will – I won't see you going back to that hospital, Sam."

"Why did you do it?!" Sam asked.

"Because I was jealous of you – you had it all. You even had Mam and Dad's approval of everything. They didn't even want me going to drama school or anything – they had me trapped. I felt suffocated. They needed to be removed from my life, which Harry helped me to see. I saw you as my scapegoat, I'm sorry," she said, wiping tears away. "That day at the hospital, I planned to break you out…"

"*What*?!" Harry blurted. "I never knew that!"

"No, because I knew you'd be mad. That's why I wanted to go there that day, but you were so irate when you saw me, Sam, that I knew there was no way I could do it, and so I was forced to leave you there."

Sam stood there, her mouth open but no words coming out. "Did you plan to leave me there to rot?"

"No, I would have come back for you, but the time had to be right. You have to believe me!" Crystal pleaded. "The last few days, all I've been able to think about is what I was going to say to you, and now it's here, all I can really say is sorry. Sorry for the whole fucking mess I've caused, and sorry for killing your parents."

"You mean *our* parents?"

"Biologically, yes, but they will never, ever be my parents. I swear I hated them from the moment I opened my eyes…"

Sam sighed. "It's all too much to take in, Crystal. You had me locked away for ten fucking years! Ten! I think it's going to take more than a few choice words and some tears to make me come around, sorry."

"Will you try? After this, we could try to move on – you could come with Harry and me?"

"Hold the fuck on," Harry said. "We've always been a double act, you know that!"

"Don't fret, Harry – I don't think I'd be interested in tagging along!" Sam said, sitting down.

The others looked at each other, unsure what to say.

"Look, this is all very touching, but can we please get on with what we came here for tonight?" Norm said, breaking the silence.

"*Oh, look at the big man!*" Angharad said.

He gave her a stiff look. "Please, love, I have to speak my mind."

"*I never knew your balls were so weighty!*"

"Sam, you have the floor," Wadsworth interrupted.

"Well," Sam began, "without really having to look at this stuff, I can see the connection here. Myself, Norm and Santa Klaws were all locked up at Castell Hirwaun together, which links us. Not only that, but our medical records are here," she said, holding them up for everyone to see. "Plus, Crystal is my sister, and Mr. Tickles and Klaws are brothers. I can only assume we were brought here due to our connections…"

"How did you know Klaws was my brother?" Mr. Tickles asked.

"Because I've spoken with him," she said. Some of the others gasped.

"But...How?"

"As I said, he was inside with me – I saw him a few times, but I thought his ramblings were that of a madman."

"Yes. Very good, Samantha. You've also appeared in a book together!" Wadsworth announced. "Some of you may have read it, others not. That's the main reason you have all been brought here..."

"A *book*?!" Norm asked.

"Yes," Wadsworth said, producing a copy of *White Walls and Straitjackets* from behind his back.

"Let me see!" Norm said.

"I've read it," Mr. Tickles said.

"Harry and I also," Crystal said. "Do you know of Shelby and Hob?"

Wadsworth turned to Crystal. "Why yes, Hob actually helped me gather everyone. Shelby would have been a guest here this evening, but he seems to have gone missing..."

Crystal looked away from the butler, not wanting to give anything away.

"How did the writer know so much about us?" Norm asked.

"I'm getting to that," Wadsworth said. "Have any of you managed to work it out yet?"

"No," Crystal said.

Mr. Tickles shook his head, along with Norm.

"What about you, Sam?"

"I don't know what to think – my head is spinning!"

"Well, stop it spinning!" Wadsworth said. "It's time I took you all into the dining room to meet your host."

"Will the host give us all the answers we seek?" Crystal asked.

"Oh, I'm sure your host will be more than happy to divulge all the information you're after!"

"Well, what the hell are we waiting for? Let's go and have dinner with our host!" Mr. Tickles said, which was followed by a robust burst of laughter.

"Yes, quite!" Wadsworth said. "Please, if you could all follow me."

THE DINNER

As they crossed the hallway from the sitting room to the dining room, something suddenly struck Crystal: Nobody's shoes were making a sound on the stone flooring. She found that odd, as her heels should have been clacking along the ground – so too should have Sam's, but no footfalls could be heard.

Stopping, she looked closer at the floor, but couldn't work it out. She stomped her foot a few times, but still no sound came. Bending, she reached out and touched the floor, but drew her hand back sharply – it felt fake. Much like a wall does when you tap it.

With walls in mind, she went to the nearest one and tapped on it. Just like the floor, it was fake. "What the…?" she said, looking about her. She thought she'd try the stairs, but when she got there she realised the whole staircase and back of the house was fake as well.

It was nothing more than a backdrop.

Like a backdrop to a theatre stage, she thought. "What's going on, Harry?!"

"I don't know, but I'm not liking it!"

"*Uh-hmm!*"

Turning, she saw Wadsworth standing by the door to the dining area, his bodyguards in tow.

"Would you like to join the rest of us?" he asked.

For the first time, she heard it – the sound of keys, as though someone was working away on a typewriter. When a series of clicks were followed by a ding, Crystal knew that's exactly what she was hearing.

Reluctantly, she nodded. "Okay," she said, following the butler.

The closer they got to the dining room door, the louder the clicking sounds became. It started to sound like thunder in her ears – tears started to roll down her cheeks, as she feared the worst.

"It'll be all right, Crystal – I'm here with you!" Harry said. "And whatever happens, we will face it together."

She held him tighter, and tighter still as she got to the dining room door and looked in. The other guests parted like the Red Sea, giving her a perfect view of the person sat at the plush-looking table.

A typewriter and a pint of beer were set before him. When she latched eyes with the big bearded man, she knew him…"*David!*"

He looked up at her and then pushed his glasses back up the bridge of his nose. His long hair, which flanked his face, hung loose – he looked as though he hadn't slept in days. "Hello, Crystal. It's nice to finally meet you!" he said. "I have to say, you look much better in the flesh than you do inside my head. As a matter of fact, you all do!"

"What in the fuck is going on here?" Sam asked. She looked back at Crystal, but all Crystal could do was shrug her shoulders.

David took a sip of his beer before talking. "Come, Crystal. You know exactly what's going on, don't you?"

he said. "Haven't you been having dreams about me? Haven't you all? Take a good look at my face and tell me you haven't!"

"You seem familiar, that's for sure," Mr. Tickles confessed.

"You've been in my dreams," Norm said.

"Mine, too," Sam confirmed.

"Good, because you've all been in my mind for years. I haven't been able to get rid of you!" David said.

"You wrote *White Walls*, didn't you?" Crystal asked.

He smiled, letting a chuckle escape. "Of course I did. I even gave myself a small cameo."

"How do you know so much about us?" Norm asked.

David turned to the lumberjack. "Haven't you worked it out?"

"Worked what out?" Norm demanded.

"*You?*" David asked Mr. Tickles, who shook his head.

"It's all very simple. I *created* you – you're nothing more than fictional characters. All of you. Even Wadsworth."

"I can see why you were in the loony bin now!" Sam said, sniggering. "You might be able to fool the rest of them, but not me." Stepping up to him, she got into his face. "I remember seeing you at the hospital."

David smiled. "Of course you do – I planted that memory in your mind, much like I made you a victim and everything else that's been going on. It's all written here!" he said gleefully, pointing at the stack of paper by the side of the typewriter.

"What is it?" Mr. Tickles asked.

"*Escapees and Fevered Minds* – the sequel to *White Walls*," he said.

"You're talking through your arse!" Mr. Tickles said.

"Oh, I'm afraid not. You're nothing more than words on paper! And I can prove it – I could tell you things about yourselves that not even you know," he said, and then he reeled off personal information about each and every one of them.

"This can't be true!" Sam said.

"I think it is," Crystal said, wiping a tear off her cheek. "My whole life has been...*fake*?" she asked.

"You've not lived a life, Crystal – it's all in your bogus head," David said. "I brought you all here to tell you that."

"Where are we?" Mr. Tickles asked.

"In a corner of my imagination," David said.

"But the breakout? The newspaper reports...?" Norm said.

"What about them?"

"It's all too real to be..."

David shook his head. "It's all fiction. Every step you've made to get this far has been written by me. All your thoughts, activities, meals, fears and movements were written days and days ago."

"If this is true, why bring us here to tell us that? There must be more to it?!" Crystal demanded.

"Yes, there is – I want to kill you all off!" David said. "I don't normally write sequels, but I felt I was obliged to. Some of you – mainly you, Crystal – have plagued my mind, have yearned to be written about again. But it ends here. Tonight!"

"You and whose fucking army, pal?!" Mr. Tickles asked.

"I don't need an army – I have a badass on standby!" David said, stepping away from the typewriter.

"Where the fuck do you think you're going?!" Sam asked.

"Just moving to a safer area..." he said, smiling.

Mr. Tickles opened his mouth to speak, but an explosion of glass from behind quieted him. He, Norm, Crystal, Sam and both Sideshows turned around.

Through the shower of glass came a large box wrapped in brightly coloured paper, complete with bow and tag. Instead of hitting the floor, it landed in Mr. Tickles' hands. Immediately he could hear ticking coming from within it.

BOOM!

The huge blast tore the clown, Norm, Angharad and Sideshow Necrotic asunder – their blood, guts and hunks of bone plastered the walls, floor and table. Sideshow Nightshade screamed as a chunk of shrapnel lodged in her shoulder, causing her to go to ground.

Crystal and Sam were both thrown to the floor, the bang ringing in their ears. Crystal could only watch as David and Wadsworth slipped out the dining room door, along with the bodyguards.

"Filthy bastard!" she screamed.

Pushing Harry to safety under the table, she got to her knees and made her way over to Sam, who was bleeding from the nose and ears. "Are you okay? Can you stand?"

Sam nodded but winced as she got into a sitting position.

"Ho-ho-ho! Merry Christmas!" a voice yelled behind them.

Looking over her shoulder, Crystal saw Klaws walk through the ruptured window – most of the wall had collapsed under the abnormity of the bomb's destruction. He held in his hands a giant fire axe, which he raised above his head. "Time to die, just like all naughty children!" he said.

Before he could bring the axe down on Crystal and her sister, Sideshow Nightshade stepped in and rammed a knife into the man's shoulder – his blood spurted wildly as he staggered about the room.

"*Argh!*" he yelled, bounding off a wall.

"Quick, let's go!" Nightshade said, helping Crystal get Sam off the floor.

Fire had started to climb the walls, and thick smoke engulfed them. The house groaned and creaked as the flames started to consume it.

"Bitch!" Klaws yelled, swinging the axe at Nightshade, who was forced to let go of Sam to avoid a hit to the face.

"No!" Crystal yelled, letting her sister's other arm go and jumping on Klaws' back. The black Santa staggered around the room as he tried to dislodge her.

This gave Nightshade a perfect opportunity to knee Klaws in the balls.

"*Ooaf!*" he groaned, dropping the axe and clutching his nuts.

Whilst he nursed his privates, Crystal dug her fingers into his eyes and pushed.

"*Argh!*" he screamed, bucking wildly.

His shaking was so violent that he managed to throw Crystal off his back and also avoided the axe Nightshade was swinging at his head. The force of her missed swing took her off-kilter, allowing Klaws to wrap his hands around her throat. He squeezed with all his might before throwing her out the dining room window.

With his back turned, Klaws failed to see Crystal rush him with two forks from off the table. She punched them into his back. He let out a howl as he tried to reach around to pull them free.

"Now you're fucked!" Crystal said, picking Harry up off the floor and putting him in the crux of her arm.

Harry unleashed a flurry of throwing stars, with three hitting Klaws in the face – a fourth and fifth sank into the man's neck and throat. He fell against the wall behind him, and then slid down it.

"If we don't get out of here soon, the whole place is going to go!" Harry said.

"I need to get my sister!" Crystal said.

"Fuck that bitch!" Harry said. "She'll only turn on you later."

"We don't know that!" Going to Sam, Crystal helped her to her feet. "Come on, we have to get out of here!"

Sam groaned.

As Crystal turned to face the window, she was shocked to see Klaws rush her. Jumping to one side, she avoided his tackle with success, but he managed to shoulder charge Sam onto the dining table.

Looking back, Crystal saw Klaws trying to throttle her sister.

"We have to go!" Harry said.

"No, I can't le—"

A loud cracking sound cut her off, and she witnessed the ceiling above Sam and Klaws give way as the roof fell through. Huge chunks of brick smashed down on their heads and bodies, which was enough to kill them both.

Getting to the outside, Crystal was shocked to find Nightshade still alive. They coughed and wheezed as they watched the building fall through.

"Where's your sister?"

"Dead!" Crystal said.

"You don't seem too unhappy about it," Nightshade said. "What about that grand apology?"

"A truce would never have lasted – I'm sure she would have tried to kill me."

"I guess we'll never know."

"No. I guess that's the end of everything!" Crystal said.

"I was almost firewood!" Harry said.

"That was never going to happen," Crystal said. "I would have died with you had you been killed."

"Now what?" Nightshade asked.

"What do you mean?"

"David's still out there, and he's not going to stop until we're dead – he'll just write us into another trap. We can't escape. We can't win!"

"Do you think we were meant to survive that blast?"

"Probably not. And if we had, I'm sure David was hoping Klaws would finish us off," Nightshade said. "We could just slip away – nobody will be any of the wiser?"

"Are these even our own thoughts?" Crystal asked. "He would never let us just 'slip away.' Never."

Nightshade shook her head. "I say we get back to the circus. We can leave with it tomorrow."

"What about Mr. Tickles?" Crystal asked.

"I can explain things – don't worry, you and Harry will be safe."

Without another word, all three fled the scene, heading back to the fairground.

THE AFTERMATH

The next day the circus pulled out of Porthcawl with Crystal and Harry stowed away. They had plenty of unanswered questions on their minds, which they spoke of between themselves.

Are we out of danger?

Will the writer let us go?

Will he lead us somewhere else?

If he knows we are alive, will he write about us again?

These are questions to which they will never know the answers – will never be privy to. Why? Because I can't have my characters, or readers, knowing their fate. That would be madness!

When I wrote the end to *Escapees and Fevered Minds*, I knew exactly who would live and who would die. I'm quite happy to allow Crystal, Harry and Nightshade to keep on living for now – at least I managed to kill off a few of the others, which has freed up a bit of space inside my mind.

Will I turn the series into a trilogy? Who knows! Maybe you, the reader, can figure out how it all ends?

Is Harry real?

Maybe…

All I do know is that my characters are still out there, appearing in a circus of utter horrors. Pray they never come to a town near you…

But they are all in your mind, I hear you say, dear author?

That might be true, but how do you know for certain…?!

About Your Author

David Owain Hughes is a horror freak! He grew up on ninja, pirate and horror movies from the age of five, which rapidly instilled in him a vivid imagination. When he grows up, he wishes to be a serial killer with a part-time job in women's lingerie…

He's had multiple short stories published in various online magazines and anthologies, along with articles, reviews and interviews. He's written for This Is Horror, Blood Magazine, and Horror Geeks Magazine. He's the author of the popular novels "Walled In" (2014), "Wind-Up Toy" (2016), "Man-Eating Fucks" (2016), and "The Rack & Cue" (2017) along with his short story collections "White Walls and Straitjackets" (2015) and "Choice Cuts" (2015). He's also written three novellas – "Granville" (2016), "Wind-Up Toy: Broken Plaything & Chaos Rising" (2016).

www.hellboundbookspublishing.com/authorpage_hughes.html

www.facebook.com/DOHughesAuthor/?ref=hl

www.amazon.co.uk/David-Owain-Hughes/e/B00L708P2M/ref=sr_ntt_srch_lnk_3?qid=145

8241417&sr=1-3

http://david-owain-hughes.wix.com/horrorwriter

www.goodreads.com/author/show/4877205.David_O
wain_Hughes

twitter.com/DOHUGHES32

ALSO BY DAVID OWAIN HUGHES...
<u>Available at: www.hellboundbookspublishing.com</u>

Whitewalls and Straitjackets

Meet Crystal and Harry - sweethearts and lovers who work in the salubrious fringes of the entertainment business.

After brutally murdering three critics for poor reviews of their show, Crystal and Harry decide it best to skip town and head for the coast. Once there, they know that everything will turn out just fine - it will be their chance to start afresh.

A new beginning.

But, before they make their way to the seaside, Crystal insists that they visit her sister at Castell Hirwaun, the renowned psychiatric facility for the dangerously insane - since, after all, it is because of Crystal that her sibling sits rotting in the place.

At the beginning of their adventure, Harry discovers a book in the van's glove compartment - *Whitewalls and Straightjackets* - written by an unknown author who exhibits the most intimate knowledge of the deadly duo, along with the other nut jobs who lurk within the Rhonda Valleys in that most picturesque part of South Wales.

As lives and stories collide head-on, Crystal and Harry soon realize that escaping the Valleys won't be quite as easy as they'd first assumed - especially so with another vicious serial killer hot on their heels....

Man Eating F*cks

A dark, incredibly entertaining excursion into the delightfully twisted imagination of David Owain Hughes....

An average teenage girl and her father find themselves caught up in a brutal nightmare at their local recreational centre, when an age-old enemy comes stumbling out of the woods to crash a heavy-metal gig; a gig that has all the promises of being killer. This is one blood-soaked gig you won't want to miss!

Praise for Man-Eating F*cks from Ty Schwamberger (author of The Fields, Deep Dark Woods & The Death of a Horror Writer.) *"Man Eating F*cks is old school horror, but with a new, blood-soaked twist! David Owain Hughes effectively creates enjoyable and lethal characters in this tale that is sure to keep you up at night. This is the type of tale that you need to read with a light on...I'm serious. You better put your seatbelt on 'cause you're in for one helluva ride. Look out, Hughes might very well be headed to the major leagues after this twisted tale! Highly recommended!"*

Man Eating F*ckers

The eagerly awaited sequel to Hughes' critically acclaimed *Man Eating F**ks...*

Two years on from her nightmarish descent into the woods, Storm is piecing her life back together, but trouble is forming...

A new threat is rising - one that promises to grip, shake and spin Storm's world out of control. But that's not all, as a 'friend' and sympathizer also poses a risk from the shadows, combined with a face from the past...

With the cannibals lurking in the background, waiting for an opportunity to deal white-hot vengeance, can father and daughter survive?

** Features a bonus, previously unpublished short story by David Owain Hughes**

David Owain Hughes

Psychological Breakdown

Within this tome lies eighteen tales of mind-bending terror, as Hughes delves into the human psyche and dishes out stories of what becomes of the broken minded, spirited and downright irked.

Part these blood-drenched pages at your own peril, for you will find diseased minds geared towards revenge and bloody chaos, with a few twists, turns and surprises thrown in for good, fucked-up measures.

Keep the lights on!

Puckered

Percy is kinky.
Percy is perverted.
Percy is a loner.
Percy is sneaky…

…But most of all, Percy wants to be left alone.

Whether it be a nagging mother or something from his past, it feels like he is always trying to escape something.

Will he be able to find his own peace, or will the real world catch up to him?

There will be blood.

There will be s**t.

There will be unusual sexual kinks.

But most of all, there will be murder…

<u>Other HellBound Books Titles</u>

<u>Available at: www.hellboundbookspublishing.com</u>

Worship Me

Something is listening to the prayers of St. Paul's United Church, but it's not the god they asked for; it's something much, much older.

A quiet Sunday service turns into a living hell when this ancient entity descends upon the house of worship and claims the congregation for its own. The terrified churchgoers must now prove their loyalty to their new god by giving it one of their children or in two days time it will return and destroy them all.

As fear rips the congregation apart, it becomes clear that if they're to survive this untold horror, the faithful must become the faithless and enter into a battle against God itself. But as time runs out, they discover that true monsters come not from heaven or hell... ...they come from within.

No Rest For The Wicked

A modern day ghost story with its skeletons buried firmly in the past. From beyond the grave, a murderous wife seeks to complete her revenge on those who betrayed her in life; a powerless domestic still fears for her immortal soul while trying to scare off anyone who comes too close; and the former plantation master - a sadistic doctor who puts more faith in the teachings of de Sade than the Bible

When Eric and Grace McLaughlin purchase Greenbrier Plantation, their dreams are just as big as those who have tried to tame the place before them. But, the doctor has learned a thing or two over his many years in the afterlife, is putting those new skills to the test, and will go to great lengths in order to gain the upper hand. While Grace digs into the death-filled history of her new home, Eric soon becomes a pawn of the doctor's unsavory desires and rapidly growing power, and is hell-bent on stopping her.

The Amnesia Girl

Filled with copious amounts of black humor, Gerri R. Gray's first published novel is an offbeat adventure story that could be described as One Flew over the Cuckoo's Nest meets Thelma and Louise.

Flashback to 1974. Farika is a lovely young woman who wakes up one day to find herself a patient in a bizarre New York City psychiatric asylum. She has no idea who she is, and possesses no memories of where she came from nor how she got there.

Fearing for her life after being attacked by a berserk girl with over one hundred personalities and a vicious nurse with sadistic intentions, the frightened amnesiac teams up with an audacious lesbian with a comically unbalanced mind, and together they attempt a daring escape.

But little do they know that a long strange journey into an even more insane world filled with a multitude of perilous predicaments and off-kilter individuals are waiting for them on the outside. Farika's weird reality crumbles when she finally discovers who, and what, she really is!

The Cabin Sessions

The Cabin Sessions is a confronting, hard-hitting dark psychological thriller, told with an acid wit. Themes of domestic and child abuse are explored through minds distorted by fear, and corrupted by hatred and delusion. A tale where redemption is gained in unexpected ways.

It's Christmas Eve when hapless musician Adam Banks stands on the bridge over the river that cleaves the isolated village of Burton. A storm is rolling into the narrow mountain pass. He thinks of turning back. Instead, he resolves to fulfill his obligation to perform the guest spot at The Cabin Sessions. He should be looking forward to it, but fear stirs when he opens the door on the Cabin's incense-choked air.

Meanwhile, Philip's sister, Eva, prepares to take a bath. It's a ritual. She's a breath holder. At twenty-eight she's returned to Burton to finish the business of her past; business she must attend to, if only she could make sense of it. Memories begin to surface concerning the innocence of her brother.

Blood and Kisses

The definitive short story collecting from James H Longmore - an eclectic mix of dark horror, bizarro and Twilight-Zone style tales of the downright disturbing.

Welcome to the long awaited collection from the writer of horror novels *'Pede* and *Tenebrion*; a forword by Richard Chizmar (co-author of *Gwendy's Button Box* and author of *A Long December*), 18 short stories, 5 flash fiction and even a poem - all skin-crawling, soul-shredding tales of terror, of the darkest things that skulk amongst the night's inky shadows, and of the everyday gone horribly awry.

Discover the alternative implication of technology becoming self-aware, enjoy the acquaintance of a charismatic new pastor who promises his flock a brand new place in which to worship his God, and spend a little time in the company of a nice young man who is inexorably caught up in his home town's terrible secret. Then there is Cupid's revelation that personally he has never experienced love, yet we discover that very emotion alive and not so well amongst the ruins of a post zombie apocalypse world, and we bear witness to a childhood innocence forever destroyed in a war-torn city. There is more, Dear Reader, much, much more; for within these pages we have devils, demons and ghosts, lycanthropes and demi-gods, all rubbing nefarious shoulders with vilest of Hell's offspring who have slithered from the netherworld to doff their caps and wish us all the sweetest of dreams…

The Big Book of Bootleg Horror 2

The second volume in HellBound Books' flagship horror anthology - this one bursting at the seams with even more fantastically dark horror from the cream of the rising stars in today's horror scene!

Featuring: Tracey A. Cross, Elizabeth Zemlicka, Shelby Thomas, Matthew Gillies, Spinster Eskie, Stephen Clements, Ken Goldman, Nathan Robinson, K.M. Campbell, Cody Grady, Sebastian Bendix, Leo X. Robertson, David Owain Hughes, Timothy McGivney, Kane Gordon, Todd Sullivan, Mike Mayak, Edward Ahern, Rose Garnett, Jaap Boekestein, Brandy Delight, Stanley B. Webb, D. Norfolk, and Thomas Gunther.

**A HellBound Books LLC
Publication**

http://www.hellboundbookspublishing.com

Printed in the United States of America